"Let me go!"

He ignored her, saying, "We're going back to the car."

"You'll have to carry me first," she retorted, digging in her heels.

"Right." Sinclair decided to take her literally. Tiree was a very slight figure, five foot four with a slim build—no problem to a man almost a head taller and with a muscular physique.

"Hold on to me." He bent an arm around her shoulders and knees to lift her clean off her feet.

He didn't like this girl. She wasn't his type. But none of these factors stopped his body reacting to her proximity. She looked at him with those wide green eyes of hers. He noticed, for the first time, a face so naturally beautiful it made him forget all the other things about her and obey his baser instincts. He lowered his mouth to hers....

MISTRESS
TO A
MILLIONAIRE

*She's his in the bedroom,
but he can't buy her love...*

Another steamy title
in this
Harlequin Presents® series
is coming next month!

The Italian's Trophy Mistress (#2321)
by
Diana Hamilton

Alison Fraser

HIS MISTRESS'S SECRET

MISTRESS
To A
MILLIONAIRE

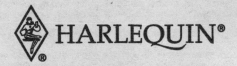

HARLEQUIN®

TORONTO • NEW YORK • LONDON
AMSTERDAM • PARIS • SYDNEY • HAMBURG
STOCKHOLM • ATHENS • TOKYO • MILAN • MADRID
PRAGUE • WARSAW • BUDAPEST • AUCKLAND

ISBN 0-373-12317-5

HIS MISTRESS'S SECRET

First North American Publication 2003.

CHAPTER ONE

EWAN SINCLAIR—Sinc to his friends—poured himself a whisky and sat down at his desk. The inquest was over, closed, the verdict in. A tragic accident, with no one to blame.

What a joke! He could think of at least three people indirectly responsible for Kit's death.

There was himself, for a start. He was the closest Kit had ever had to a father yet Kit hadn't felt able to turn to him in his time of trouble. Maybe the boy had feared he'd give him a lecture. Maybe he would have. He would never know. Death didn't allow re-runs.

Then there was Stuart Maclennan. It had been impossible to establish whether they'd been racing or pursuing each other when bike and car had gone off the road. Either way, Maclennan had been the one drugged up and so culpable in Sinc's eyes.

Finally there was Ti Nemo, Kit's erstwhile girlfriend. Sinclair had watched her on the witness stand, all peroxide hair and too much make-up. Loathing her on sight, he'd strained to catch the lies that had dropped from that pout of a mouth. He'd wanted to leap from the public gallery and shake her until she stopped repeating, parrot fashion, the story some clever lawyer had concocted for her.

But, of course, he had just sat, the habit of restraint too ingrained.

He imagined his ex-wife, Nicole, mocking him from her grave. Inhibited, repressed, incarcerated in an emotional straitjacket. Those were some of the politer insults his ex-wife had hurled at him. He hadn't much cared at the time, but they came back to haunt him now.

He needed to do something, but what?

He opened a drawer and took out Kit's effects. A plastic bag with a ring, leather wristband and broken watch, handed over by the police. Not much to show for nineteen years on this earth. He fingered each item in turn but felt no connection.

The only other possession he had of Kit's was his mobile phone, found in the glove compartment of Maclennan's car. He'd had to buy a charger for it. He knew it might be the key to his stepson's life—and subsequent death—but he had yet to try it.

He'd been waiting for the judicial process to run its course, although now he wondered what he'd been hoping for. Some reason he could accept for his stepson taking a hairpin bend at ninety? Naïve, of course. Two of the players were dead and the third had claimed ignorance. If he wanted the truth, he'd have to find it himself.

He reached for the mobile and pressed the on/off switch. The display illuminated, requesting a code. He had three chances, at most, to get it right.

He tried the last four digits of Kit's old flat number and the year of his birth. Both came up, 'CODE INCORRECT'. Last guess, his birthdate, and he was staring at the words, 'CODE ACCEPTED'.

Another person would have seen it as fate. Sinclair thought it just luck and wasn't sure if it was good or bad, as he began to search the mobile's directory.

It didn't take him long. There she was. First slot: TN. Second slot: TN Mobile. Who else but Ti Nemo, ridiculous name that it was? Her top billing spoke volumes about who was important to Kit at the time of his death.

Sinclair hesitated briefly, then for once let impulse rule as he pressed the dial button.

Tiree Nemo was pouring a second glass of wine at almost the same moment as Ewan Sinclair, twenty miles away, was pouring his first whisky. She wasn't a drinker but she needed to dull the edges of the traumatic day, and, for that matter, the fourteen days that had preceded it.

No, she certainly wasn't a drinker. Another couple of sips and she was light-headed. It probably didn't help that she had yet to eat that day.

She leaned back against the sofa and tried to think of nothing. Not the coroner's court, nor the Press desperate for a story, nor the fans reaching out to comfort or be comforted.

What a circus it had been: bulbs popping, arms jostling, voices clamouring for her attention. Look this way, Ti. Over here, Ti. How do you feel? A few words for the fans?

Suddenly they were the height of fame. If only Stu had been there. He would have loved it, posing and posturing, pretending indifference even as he played up to the audience.

Not Kit, of course. He would have hung back as he always did, looking as if he wanted to disappear altogether. Painfully shy for a rock star. Or maybe just painfully young.

That was the real sin they'd committed, allowing a seventeen-year-old to join the band. A succession of experienced guitarists had auditioned for them, and they'd gone for an insecure schoolboy. True, Kit had played a wicked bass, but hadn't it been obvious almost from the outset that he'd never cope with the fame?

'What did we do, Stu?' She actually asked the question aloud.

Leave off, Mouse, the answer came back in her head, *you can't take me on your guilt trip. I'm dead too, remember.*

As if she could forget.

You're not going to cry or anything.

No!

Good, because that would be really boring.

Tiree pulled a face at this final comment from Stu before she realised she was doing it again. Having conversations with a dead person. She sealed her lips tightly, knowing that if she replied, it would carry on until Stu had the last word as always.

She didn't think she was going mad. She'd just spent half her life with Stu somewhere in the background, observing, commenting, controlling, and it was hard to live in a vacuum.

Not that she was short of invitations to confide. Far from it. The dailies, the glossies and a host of women's magazines were vying to publish the headline: TI TALKS ABOUT TERRIBLE TRAGEDY.

She was so tired of their calls she'd begun to hang up mid-sentence. Sometimes she didn't even bother picking up the telephone. Such as now, when it rang.

She turned her head and stared at the handset, wondering how long before the person lost interest and rang off. Most took three or four minutes before they accepted she was neither going to answer nor allow them the chance to talk into a machine.

This particular caller was more persistent. The ringing seemed endless before it cut abruptly, only to recommence almost immediately. She suspected it was Les, the band manager, but she had no wish to speak to him, either.

At length she picked up the receiver and, severing the connection, dialled up the speaking clock. She noted the precise time before laying the phone down on the table. Now any caller would have to be satisfied with a continuously engaged signal.

She leaned back again, trying to blank her mind, but thoughts kept chasing round and round in pointless circles, driving her crazy, as was the mechanical voice informing her of the seconds passing.

She suffered another fifteen minutes of it before hanging up the line. The telephone stayed mercifully silent. The thoughts in her head did not.

She rose to her feet and had to steady herself slightly against the effects of the wine. It was only eight o'clock but perhaps if she lay down on her bed, sleep would come.

She walked out into the hall and gripped hard on the handrail as she climbed up the steep, windy staircase. She'd barely entered her bedroom when the ringing began again. A different sound this time, more a trilling, lower in pitch and volume. It came from the mobile abandoned amid a clutter of wigs and clothes on the bed.

She picked it up and pressed the reject-call button, but not before her brain registered the words: *Kit's mobile.*

Kit's mobile? How could it be?

A little shaken, she walked to the phone by her bed and dialled 1471 on this landline. The same number, Kit's, came back at her. But how?

Her mind went in flashback to *the* night. Kit gathering his things, zipping up his bike leathers, too tight to accommodate much. What had he done with his mobile? Nothing. Stu had picked it up instead.

Had it really survived the crash? Stu's car had been a mangled wreck, but it was possible. The question was who had it now?

Tiree decided not to make a mystery of it and pressed her redial button.

The call was answered almost instantly.

'Yes, who is this?' a male voice, cool and cultured, enquired.

'You dialled my number.' Tiree put the onus on him to do the talking.

'Ti Nemo?'

'Miss Nemo is not in residence. Can I take a message?'

The lie was automatic. She'd had crank calls in the past, fans who had somehow discovered her number, forcing her to change it with annoying frequency.

'This is Kit Harrison's father,' she was informed after a lengthy pause.

Tiree was initially shocked, then cross as she realised she wasn't the only one lying. Kit hadn't said much about his parents, but she knew his mother was dead and his American father might as well have been, having ignored Kit's existence for most of his nineteen years.

'You can't be,' she replied bluntly. 'Kit's father was American.'

'Granted,' the upper-class English voice came back. 'I should have said I'm—was Kit's *step*father.'

Tiree supposed that could be true. Kit had had several stepfathers, official and unofficial, one of whom he still contacted from time to time.

'So?' the one word was hardly encouragement.

'I'd like to talk to you,' he persisted.

Tiree decided to maintain her pretence. 'To Miss Nemo,' she corrected, 'unfortunately she's rest—'

'Please,' he cut across her, tone restrained. 'I can identify accents, too, Miss Nemo. West coast Scots, if I'm not mistaken. North of Glasgow. The Argyll peninsula, perhaps.'

He was spot on. That was unusual. Most English people couldn't pinpoint her dialect beyond Scots.

Tiree gave up on denial and demanded brusquely, 'Look, what do you want?'

'I have some questions about Kit that you may be able to answer,' he resumed. 'If it's convenient, I'd like to come and see you.'

'Now?'

'Preferably. I'm quite close.'

'Close?' she echoed. 'Close to where?'

'Your cottage,' he said slowly, as if he was stating the obvious.

Tiree registered two things simultaneously—his words and the car engine in the background—and felt a frisson of panic.

'You know where I live?' It was meant to be a secret to everyone but the band, her manager and the record company.

'I believe so,' he replied evenly. 'Kit gave me a last contact address—Ivy Cottage, Woodside Lane, near…'

Tiree didn't listen to the rest, not after the first part proved correct. Instead she went into full panic mode, remembering too well the last time an uninvited guest had made his way to her door.

'Don't come here. Do you hear me?' He couldn't fail to, as she almost yelled it, while racing towards the stairs. 'I'm calling the police. I'm calling them right now.'

The latter was a somewhat inaccurate threat as, at that point, Tiree was clambering down the steep staircase on her way to check whether the bolt was drawn on her front door.

Too fast, of course, in wool socks on polished wood. Halfway and she was in freefall, tipping forwards with her own momentum as she missed the next step. She grasped for the rail but was already in mid-air, tumbling over in an inelegant feat of gymnastics, before her head made contact with something hard and unyielding as she came to land at the bottom of the stairs.

She had a few conscious seconds to note that the bolt wasn't drawn, then finally achieved the oblivion she'd earlier sought.

*   *   *

Sinc stared at the dead phone in his hand, trying to make sense of what he'd heard before the line disconnected. Hysterical ranting followed by a scream and several thumping sounds.

Perhaps the mad woman was throwing things?

Of course, she might just have fallen downstairs.

The real debate was what to do about it. Drive the last half mile to her cottage to check on her? Or go home, resolved never again to act on impulse.

He knew which course he preferred. No contest. But he was duty-bound.

He drove on.

CHAPTER TWO

TIREE woke up in clean white sheets, wearing a paper gown and suffering from the mother of all headaches. She didn't say the clichéd, 'Where am I?' because there was no one there to ask and it was pretty obvious, anyway.

She moved her arms and her legs to see if they still worked. It seemed so, although she winced from various bruises on her body. Her hand came in contact with a buzzer but she wasn't quite ready to use it. She wanted to sort out the events of last night first.

She worked backwards. Her last clear memory was tumbling down stairs and the blinding pain as her head hit solid wood or wall. She'd been rushing and slipped on a step—so much for the aesthetics of polished wood over the practicalities of plain old-fashioned carpeting.

But why had she been rushing? Something to do with the phone. She'd been hurrying to answer it? No, not that. She shut her eyes and concentrated through the headache until it finally came back. The man with Kit's mobile, reputedly his stepfather. A rather posh voice but menacing nonetheless. He'd threatened to come to the cottage and past experiences had led her to panic.

So who had rescued her? Not him, she was almost certain. She had the vaguest memory of another voice with a soothing tone and gentle hands moving her limbs. An ambulance man? Possibly, although the journey here was lost to her, too.

She turned her head to the sound of the door opening. A nurse appeared, saw she was conscious and painted on a bright smile.

'You're awake,' she declared as if Tiree might not have noticed herself. 'How are you feeling?'

Silly question. Like she'd done ten rounds in a boxing ring.

'Fine,' Tiree forced a smile in return. 'Where am I exactly?'

'The Abbey Clinic.'

'And how long have I been here?'

'Since last night, I believe,' the nurse volunteered. 'Do you remember what happened?'

Tiree nodded. 'I slipped and fell downstairs.'

'Good.' The nurse looked pleased at her lucidity. 'No bones broken, fortunately.'

'Then I can go home?' Tiree dragged herself into a sitting position, as if preparing for escape.

'No, no, not yet.' The nurse surged forward, a gentle hand pressing Tiree back on the bed. 'The doctor will have to see you first, check that you're fit to be released.'

'All right.' Tiree wanted out with minimum fuss. 'Look, is anyone aware I'm in here?'

'Your family, you mean?'

Tiree shook her head. She had no family.

'Do you know who I am?' Her tone was one of enquiry not demand. She'd never used her fame to intimidate.

'I'm sorry,' the nurse smiled apologetically, 'but you came in as an emergency and as yet we haven't had a chance to fill in a record sheet. If you're up to it, we could do that now.'

She went round to the bed head and picked up a chart. Temperature, pulse and blood pressure readings had been entered, but no personal details.

She clearly had no inkling of Tiree's identity despite Tiree's image being on the front page of several tabloids in the last week.

But then Tiree's image was just that. A blonde wig, long and strategically tousled, covered her real hair which was dark and short. The mask of make-up for public consumption was wiped off the moment she was alone. The leather gear and tarty dresses were replaced by regulation jeans and T-shirt.

A thought occurred to Tiree. If they didn't know who she was, did she actually have to tell them?

'Name?' The nurse had her pen in one hand, clipboard in the other.

'I...' Tiree was surprised how difficult it was to come up with a pseudonym on the spot.

The nurse saw her furrowed brow and came to quite the wrong conclusion. 'Are you having difficulty remembering, dear?'

Tiree took the let-out offered. 'I…um…yes.'

'Not to worry—' the nurse was all kindness and concern '—I'll just go and fetch doctor.'

Tiree watched her scuttle from the room but was alone only a matter of moments before another nurse entered, ostensibly to take her temperature once more.

Tiree was lying back against the pillows, a thermometer popped under her tongue, when a young male doctor arrived, looking harassed. He also looked about twelve which didn't exactly imbue Tiree with confidence.

'The nurse tells me you're having difficulty remembering your name.' He used a mini-telescopic to peer into Tiree's eyes.

Tiree mumbled an answer, quite unintelligible with the thermometer in her mouth.

'Sorry.' The doctor took the thermometer out and checked the reading.

Tiree assumed it was normal. 'I'd like to go. Is that possible?'

'Go?' he echoed absently. 'Go where?'

'Home.'

'Which is where?'

Tiree shook her head. She never revealed details about her cottage. She'd once been stalked to the point where she'd had to move.

'We can't discharge you,' he relayed, 'until we're sure you're going to be all right. You've had concussion, although luckily no fracture to the skull.'

He gave her a reassuring smile, then walked to the door with the nurse, saying, 'Dr Chivers needs to be appraised of her condition. Also Mr Sinclair at Bart's should be contacted, as she was his referral. Meanwhile keep an eye on her and don't distress her with too many questions.'

He spoke in hushed tones but Tiree could still hear. She wondered if he considered her mentally impaired in some way.

She wasn't. In fact, despite a thumping headache and the

occasional wince from her various bruises, Tiree felt as sharp as ever.

'Who's Mr Sinclair?' she asked the nurse when they were alone.

The nurse hesitated briefly before relaying, 'He's Head of Paediatrics at St Bartholomew's in Reading.'

'A doctor?' Tiree concluded.

'A consultant,' the nurse stressed.

Tiree remembered then that consultants get the title *Mr* rather than *Dr* in some weird reverse snobbery.

She frowned. 'Paediatrics is children, isn't it?'

'Yes, that's right.'

'So why should *he* have referred me to here?'

'I'm not exactly sure how he is involved with your case,' the nurse told her. 'You are over sixteen?'

'I'd say so,' Tiree replied drily.

She was actually twenty-three. At times, she was taken for younger, especially without makeup, but lately she'd felt a whole lot older.

'Well, never mind,' the nurse said with forced cheerfulness, 'between him and Dr Chivers, you couldn't be in better hands.'

Tiree smiled thinly. She didn't want to be in any doctor's hands, but, home, planning what she was going to do with the rest of her life.

'Do you happen to know where my clothes are?' She tried to make it sound a casual enquiry.

'I'm afraid not,' the nurse answered. 'I'll try and find out.'

'Thanks,' murmured a resigned Tiree.

Regardless of whether or not the tabloids had been alerted, she could hardly walk out of this clinic wearing a paper hospital gown which gaped at the rear.

Left alone, she lay back and tried to fill in gaps from last night. She still couldn't put a face or a name to her rescuer. The obvious person was Kit's stepfather but she was convinced it couldn't be him. If *he'd* found her, she'd be still lying at the foot of her stairs.

But who else might have called on spec? Few people knew the location of the cottage and fewer still had been welcome.

Les Gray, her manager, seemed the most likely candidate. She'd walked out on him when he'd tried to talk business after the inquest, but he was quite capable of turning up, regardless.

Tiree considered calling him now. There was a telephone on the nightstand. She knew Les, whether her rescuer or not, would drop everything and get over here with a change of clothes. Kinetic Sugar had been his main meal ticket and Kinetic Sugar was now pretty much her.

She reached for the telephone, then stopped midway. She had to think about this some more. If she told Les she was in hospital, any sympathy would be quickly superseded by speculation on how best to exploit the situation. Sure he'd hotfoot it down here, but there was every chance he'd alert the Press first.

Les lived by the adage that there was no such thing as bad publicity, and the last few weeks had proved him right. Tiree had been sick at heart when the band's last release soared to number one on the back of Stu and Kit's accident. It wouldn't have been so bad if the song had been good but it wasn't. Les, the weasel, had scarcely been able to hide his delight.

So, no, she wasn't going to call her manager.

She considered her closest girlfriend, Chrissie, but was reluctant to involve her, either. Over the last year, Chrissie had met a man, married and had a baby, and it had made a difference to their friendship despite a determination that it wouldn't. The trouble was her husband who believed he'd rescued Chrissie from bad influences like Stu and her.

Perhaps he was right, Tiree conceded. Chrissie certainly seemed happier in her domestic life.

No, she wouldn't call her.

She went through other possibilities and rejected each in turn until she finally ran out of options. She decided to bide her time and enjoy an anonymity that might prove all too brief.

The nurse came to check on her periodically. Lunch was brought and she made an effort to eat it, knowing they would note whether she did or not. Then, tired from doing nothing, she dozed off in the early afternoon.

She woke slowly, her brain switching on before her eyes

opened. She could hear voices at the foot of her bed, deep in discussion of her case, apparently requiring no input from her.

'She's stabilised?' asked the young doctor from earlier.

'I believe so, Doctor,' came from the nurse.

'Cranial damage?' a third person threw in.

His tone was abrupt and Tiree felt she should recognise it but didn't.

'No signs of it on the scan,' the doctor relayed, 'yet she appears to be suffering some identity confusion.'

'*Identity confusion*?' Mr Third Voice echoed with a slightly sarcastic inflexion.

The younger doctor quickly rephrased it. 'She doesn't seem to know her own name, sir.'

'Interesting,' was commented in a dry murmur. 'How is she behaving otherwise?'

'She's almost cheerful, considering,' the nurse contributed her own observation.

'Which is hardly normal under the circumstances,' the senior doctor responded.

'Quite,' the junior doctor agreed, 'so what do you recommend, Mr Sinclair, transferring her to General for pysch assessment of her amnesiac state?'

'That's up to Dr Chivers,' this Sinclair man said, 'she's actually his patient. I'd like to talk to her, however, if I may.'

'Certainly, sir.'

'Will I waken her, Mr Sinclair?'

Tiree, even with her eyes shut, could detect the reverence with which both junior doctor and nurse regarded *Mr* Sinclair. No wonder he sounded so arrogant. When he said, jump, they probably only stopped to ask how high.

'No need,' he drawled in upper-class English tones, 'she's awake.'

How did he know that? wondered Tiree, still with her eyes tightly shut. She sensed herself under scrutiny but remained determinedly still until long fingers wrapped round her wrist to touch the pulse point.

Only then did she let her eyes flicker open and found herself staring up at a face that didn't go with the voice and persona at all.

She had pictured an overbearing figure in his fifties with pouched eyes, pudgy cheeks and a jaw line lost in several layers of chin.

This man couldn't be more different: intensely blue eyes, cheekbones hued from granite and a mouth that, however unsmiling, could only be described as sensual. No white coat for him but the epitome of good grooming in a well-cut, grey suit that emphasised a tall, lean build.

And his age? Hard to tell; dark hair was liberally threaded with grey but the handsome face was largely unlined.

'Dr Doug Ross, as I live and breathe,' she said on the sort of impulse that often got her in trouble.

It certainly went down like a lead balloon this time. 'Who?'

'He's a character on...never mind,' she dismissed. 'You probably don't watch TV.'

'Seldom.' He breathed disapproval.

Tiree might have been quelled if she hadn't seen Florence Nightingale behind him, trying desperately not to laugh.

'You know who I am?' he added shortly.

The way *he* said the question seemed to proclaim his importance and she couldn't resist a shrugged, 'Should I?'

He frowned, before turning to the young doctor and nurse. 'Would you mind if I talk to the patient in confidence?'

'Of course not.' The doctor spoke for both and they left immediately.

Obviously, in their book, this Mr Sinclair was one important dude.

He was nobody to Tiree, however, and when he said, 'I assume you remember getting drunk and falling downstairs,' she was bolshie in her defence.

'I wasn't drunk,' she denied. 'I had a couple of glasses of wine, that's all.'

He failed to look convinced and, picking up her notes from the end of the bed, scanned them quickly before declaring, 'Your blood tests reveal that you were over the legal limit for driving.'

'So?' She couldn't believe this pompous ass. 'I wasn't driving, was I? I was in my own home, minding my own business, when...'

'When?' he prompted as she hesitated.

'When I happened to lose my footing on the stairs,' she finished flatly.

He still pursued, 'You weren't in any distress?'

What did he want—a confession that she'd thrown herself downstairs?

'No, I was fine,' she claimed airily. 'A1. Cool. Sorted...'

She trailed off at the look he gave her, of the 'we are not amused' variety.

Then, unbelievably, he countered, 'I know you're lying.'

Tiree was even a little shocked by it. She'd just suffered a concussion yet he was making no concessions for her potentially fragile condition.

'Don't they teach bedside manners at Med School any more?' she threw back at length.

Dark brows drew together but he offered no apology. Instead he took to studying her as if she were an interesting species— or possibly, subspecies, from his slightly disdainful expression.

'Look, does it matter how I felt before I fell?' she ran on. 'The point is how I am now and, apart from a headache and a few bruises, I'd say I was pretty okay, so if someone can bring me my clothes, I'll be out of here.'

'We can't release you,' he told her, 'while you're suffering from amnesia.'

Tiree saw she was in danger of boxing herself in and decided, no, she wasn't keeping up that pretence.

'That was a joke,' she dismissed. 'I know who I am.'

'And that is?' he enquired.

Tiree still didn't want to advertise her identity, but she was ready with a name now. 'Marie...Marie Baxter.'

It was the name of a friend from school in Glasgow. She used it with some confidence, certain that this man could not have recognised her, being neither a typical rock fan nor reader of tabloid newspapers.

He stared at her hard for a moment before muttering, 'An improvement, at least.'

'Sorry?' Tiree queried if she'd heard right.

He shook his head, resuming, 'Well, Miss Baxter—'

'It's Mrs actually,' Tiree found herself lying. Why, she didn't know.

'*Mrs* Baxter,' he stressed, 'having suffered a blow to the head, it is important that you be discharged into the care of someone responsible. Your husband—'

'He's dead,' Tiree cut in as she saw where the conversation was going.

His eyes narrowed on her.

Tiree realised he was trying to distinguish truth from fiction. She wished she hadn't started this.

She returned his scrutiny, hoping to out stare him. She was aware of his almost film-star good looks but more remarkable was the fierce intelligence behind the blue eyes. It was like having a hundred-watt bulb shining on her, exposing every flaw.

She finally looked away, unsettled.

When he next spoke, it was to say, 'I think we should stop playing games, Miss Nemo.'

'You know who I am?' She recalled how he'd let her dig a hole for herself.

He nodded. 'I did have some doubts last night. You look quite different without the hair and make-up.'

In fact, Sinclair still found it hard to reconcile. From outrageous rock chick to this.

This being? He wasn't sure. The short haircut and delicately boned face made her look like a starving waif, but the lips were still full, and behind large, green eyes lurked more of a brain than he'd anticipated.

'Last night?' she echoed.

'At the cottage,' he added.

Tiree was confused. She had no memory of this man.

'You were talking to someone on the telephone before your fall,' he prompted.

She nodded slowly. 'Kit's stepfather. You know him?'

'You could say that.' Sinclair was in no hurry to identify himself in case it set off another bout of hysteria.

'He sent you?' Tiree couldn't see another explanation.

'Something like that,' he confirmed.

Tiree tried to remember what Kit had said about any of his various stepfathers. Very little. No one in the band talked much about the childhoods they'd all been glad to leave behind.

He had mentioned a rich businessman—husband number two or three—whom he had detested. Was this the one? He'd be the kind of person to have a consultant on tap to clear up his dirty work.

'Don't tell me,' she suggested sarcastically, 'you play golf together.'

He frowned at the idea before replying, 'I don't play golf.'

'So what's the connection?' she pursued.

He paused before admitting, 'We were at school together.'

'Of course,' she commented, 'I should have known. Eton? Harrow? Somewhere like that?'

The question drew a stony look, then was ignored.

'Why are you so averse to meeting him?' he continued instead. 'He just wishes to ask you a few questions about the night of Kit's accident.'

'*Just*?' Tiree echoed this understatement before shaking her head. 'It was all said in court. He can buy a newspaper.'

'He would prefer the true version,' this man drawled in reply.

Tiree felt a degree of alarm.

The coroner had accepted her story that, after paying her a visit, Kit and Stu had decided to go back to London to do some studio work. Stu had been in his sports car, Kit on his new motorbike. She'd conceded the possibility they'd been racing. The coroner had declared their deaths accidental.

This man—or more precisely his friend—was the first to challenge her word.

'What are you implying?' Tiree settled on indignation as the best line of defence.

'I'm implying nothing,' he claimed. 'I am stating: I don't believe your account of that night was accurate.'

His tone was clinical, as if he had no personal feelings whatsoever. He had been sent to extract the truth from her and report back. Kit's stepfather had badly miscalculated his choice of emissary, however, if he thought she was going to unburden herself to this robot.

'Believe what you like.' She reached for the buzzer lying on the top sheet.

He guessed her intention and an arm shot out to stop her. Hard fingers encircled her wrist, tightening when she tried to pull free.

She raised surprised eyes and was even more surprised by what she saw in his. Mr Cool and Collected wasn't quite so calm beneath the surface.

'Is Kit's stepfather paying you to do this?' she challenged, 'or is this how you get your kicks, bullying defenceless women?'

'Defenceless?' It was genuinely incredulous. 'Is that how you see yourself?'

Hardly. Tiree was able to fight her corner. She'd always had to in the past. It was just difficult in her present circumstances.

'Well, I'm scarcely in a condition to retaliate, am I?' she pointed out. 'Still, when you've done with crushing my wrist bone, I'd like to ring for a nurse to help me dress and get the hell out of here.'

Sinclair caught the look of defiance she flashed him and felt a grudging admiration. He'd expected her to be hard, and she was, but she had spirit, too.

He released her hand, first moving the call button out of her range. She made a show of rubbing her wrist. He saw the red marks on it, the imprint of his fingers, and regretted the force he'd used. It was out of character for him. But then so was apologising.

'You have to be discharged,' he informed her, 'and that's dependent on your being absolutely fit.'

'I am.' Tiree ignored the headache between her eyes. Likely it was down to him rather than her fall.

'Taking the patient's word for it,' he pronounced in a sarcastic vein, 'is not something taught at Med School, either.'

Tiree pulled a face. What did he care if she was fit or not?

'We may also have to investigate the underlying cause of your accident,' he continued pompously.

'I think it's called lack of friction.'

'Excuse me?'

'Woollen sock on wooden stairs—' he wasn't the only one who could be sarcastic '—and an inability to counter the laws of gravity. Or in simple layman's terms: I slipped and fell.'

'Very funny.' He clearly wasn't laughing but there was a surprised look on his face, as if he hadn't expected her to be so articulate.

He probably equated the image of rock chick with brain-dead moron. Tiree decided to prove otherwise.

'Look, I'm quite prepared to sign a disclaimer if you're worried about litigation,' she ran on. 'That way you can abrogate responsibility.'

Sinclair narrowed his eyes this time, waking up to the fact that some of his assumptions about Ti Nemo were proving wildly wrong.

'Oops, sorry—' she gave him a look of mock apology '—there I go, slipping out of my stereotype again.'

Green eyes fixed on Sinclair, reflecting an acute intelligence. It didn't make him like her any better.

'So you're smart,' he granted.

'Believe it,' she advised.

'Which only makes it worse.'

'*It* being?'

She suspected he wasn't referring to her fall.

Sinclair shook his head. He felt like shaking her.

The trouble was he still wanted the truth from her. Recent events hadn't changed that. He'd assumed, in fact, that they'd make it easier, his having rescued her from a cold night unconscious on a hard floor.

He was tempted to point out he could have left her lying there, even after he'd spotted her through the letter box. He'd put himself at some risk, breaking and entering through a kitchen window. And once he'd gone to attend the injured girl, he'd had something of a shock, thinking it wasn't Ti Nemo, at all. This pale dark-haired creature bore no resemblance to the brash, blonde rock star.

He'd checked her vital signs, relieved to find her pulse steady. She'd stirred, groaning slightly, and he'd placed a soothing hand on her brow. When she'd lapsed back into unconsciousness, he used the phone in her living room to call an ambulance.

It was on a sideboard he'd seen the photograph—a casual but well-taken shot of Kit and Stuart Maclennan and this girl huddled together in a restaurant booth—and only then the truth had dawned on him. The prone figure in the hall *was* Ti Nemo, just a different version.

He stared at her now in the cold light of day, wondering which, if either, was real.

'So I can go?' Tiree demanded, unsettled by this silent appraisal.

'Not until my colleague, Dr Chivers, examines you,' he declared.

He'd returned to doctor mode but there was nothing sympathetic about his manner. If Tiree fancied a shoulder to cry on, it certainly wasn't going to be this man's.

He had to be the grimmest person she'd ever met, utterly lacking in charm despite his good looks.

He proved how lacking with his next comment. 'I shall be recommending, however, that your release should be conditional on a psychological evaluation.'

'What?' She actually thought it a sick joke at first and laughed.

He didn't laugh back. 'You were in rather a fraught state prior to your fall.'

Tiree shook her head in disbelief. She wasn't in a great state now, but that didn't mean she needed to see a shrink.

'Okay, that's it.' She'd had enough, and, pulling back the bedcovers, swung her legs over the side. 'I'm getting out of here and you'd better not try to stop me.'

Sinclair didn't have to try. He was simply there, ready to catch her, when she took a couple of steps and her legs buckled beneath her.

She literally fell against him, clutching at the wall of his chest, briefly grateful for the support of a strong arm round her waist before her sheer helplessness made her even madder.

'Let me go!' she commanded, pushing at his shoulders.

'So you can fall?' He finally smiled—at her ludicrousness. 'Of course, if that's what you want.'

Sinclair made to withdraw his arm and wasn't surprised she grabbed at him. He held onto her easily, she was so slight.

Yet, for all her fragility, she still acted tough. 'Take me back to bed!'

An imperiousness, Sinclair was in no hurry to obey. 'Please.'

'What?'

'Say please.'

Tiree raised disbelieving eyes to his. Her head was swimming, her left ankle hurting and he wanted to take time to teach her manners.

She seethed silently, all too aware that the cards were stacked in his favour as the stupid hospital gown, already exposing her naked back and butt to the world, threatened to slip off completely.

'*Please.*' The word was emitted through clenched teeth, more curse than politeness.

But it was judged sufficient as he helped her back towards the bed, gathering the flaps of her gown together.

She waited until she was sitting before she risked adding, 'You really are insufferable, you know.'

There was the merest tilt of a brow, and the comment, 'Funny, my ex-wife used to say that, too.'

He was clearly unmoved by their joint opinion. Tiree noted the 'ex' without surprise. Who could live with anyone this cold and superior?

'So, what hurts?' He'd seen her wince as she levered herself back into bed.

'My ankle,' she admitted grudgingly. 'The left one.'

Cool hands lifted her foot and began to rotate it. He was unexpectedly gentle.

Sinclair watched her face as he moved it this way and that.

She was quite a stoic character, making no sound apart from an occasional, sharp intake of breath.

'I don't think there's a break,' he assessed. 'My guess is a sprain, but we'll have it X-rayed just in case. Meanwhile I suggest you get some more sleep until the effects of the concussion wear off.'

Tiree gave him a resentful look but no longer felt up to arguing.

He drew the cover back over her legs, then retreated to the door, turning to say, 'I think you should know. I'm not a go-between.'

'What do you mean?'

'I'm the man himself.'

It was a moment before Tiree caught on.

'You're Kit's stepfather?'

'One of them, anyway.'

He smiled, the merest baring of teeth, enjoying her confusion, before he stepped smartly from the room.

Perhaps he imagined she'd throw something. It was tempting. Why hadn't he confessed earlier who he was?

And why hadn't she realised? The accent was the same, upper-class English. The voice was as cold and precise, with just that hint of menace. He was also too arrogant to be anybody's mouthpiece.

The door reopened and she glared, until she saw it was the nurse from earlier.

'Mr Sinclair thought you might need some painkillers.' She held out a little plastic cup containing two tablets.

'How considerate.' Tiree didn't mean it.

But the nurse smiled in response, as she emptied the pills into her hand.

Tiree peered at them, suspiciously. What if they were more potent than aspirin, a truth drug—for instance? Fanciful, admittedly, but that's what he was after, wasn't it? The blow-by-blow of the night of the accident.

The trouble was he wouldn't like it. He wouldn't like it one bit.

CHAPTER THREE

THE next doctor Tiree saw was a great deal more sympathetic. He arrived late afternoon and introduced himself as Dr Chivers. She was on her guard, thinking he might be there to conduct an evaluation on her mental state, but his examination was strictly physical.

He looked at the bump on the back of her head, shone a torch into her eyes and tested her reflexes. They had quite an amicable chat while he was doing this, then he pronounced her fit for release, an X-ray of her ankle having discounted anything more than a mild sprain.

Tiree felt a sense of triumph as she imagined Sinclair returning for another visit to find her gone.

Sinclair was far less pleased when Bob Chivers told him, 'I'm sorry but we can't keep her here.'

'Why not?'

'Well, to put it simply, Sinc, she's well enough to be released and we're not a hotel.'

'Do you need the bed?' Sinclair asked. 'Because if you don't, keep her another couple of nights and I'll pay her fee.'

'You know it isn't money,' his friend appeased. 'If she actually wished to stay, that would be different. We could keep her in for observation. But she doesn't. Provided she has someone to supervise her for the next twenty-four hours, I see no reason she can't go home.'

Sinclair saw he wasn't going to move Bob on this score and tried another. 'Yes, all right, I accept she's physically fit enough to leave, but have you considered her psychological state? Didn't she strike you as unbalanced?'

'Actually, no. Quirky, maybe,' Bob conceded, 'but, in light of recent events—the accident, the coroner's court and now this fall—she's coping rather well. In fact, I'm more concerned about you, Sinc.'

'Thanks.'

'I'm serious. I know it's been hard to accept Kit's death, but I doubt anything that girl could tell you, will make you feel better.'

'I don't want to feel better,' Sinclair echoed uncompromisingly. 'I just want the truth.'

Bob shook his head, giving up. 'Well, I'll let you talk to her once more before she leaves. Just go easy. She's still a patient.'

'Yes, of course,' Sinclair agreed, already heading towards the door.

'And perhaps a little charm might not go amiss,' Bob called after him.

Absurd advice when applied to Ti Nemo, but Sinclair raised a hand in acknowledgement, letting Bob think he might actually comply.

He walked from Bob's office to the nurses' station, announcing his intention of visiting the patient. The sister confirmed that she was dressed while a couple of the auxiliaries awarded him curious looks which he chose to ignore.

He knocked briefly before he entered the room.

Wearing last night's clothes of jeans and T-shirt, Tiree was sitting in a wheelchair, waiting for release. A light support bandage had been put on her ankle and she was wearing sandals borrowed from the nursing staff, having arrived at the hospital without footwear.

'Oh, it's you,' she said, on seeing him.

It was not an inspiring start to a conversation far less a charm offensive.

He tried, however, managing a concerned, 'How's the ankle?'

She shrugged. 'I'll live... Sorry to disappoint.'

He took a deep breath. No, this wasn't going to be easy.

'I'm afraid we got off on the wrong foot,' he said in a conciliatory tone. 'I just wish to talk. I don't quite know why I panicked you last night—'

'A complete stranger rings me late at night,' she cut in,

'claims he's Kit's dad and tells me he's about to arrive on my doorstep, and you don't know why that would make me a little nervous?'

'Eight o'clock is scarcely late,' he countered, 'I *am* Kit's dad—well, as much as anyone was—what did you think, that I was going to force my way into your cottage? You overreacted.'

She was silent for a moment and Sinc actually imagined she'd taken on board what he'd just said, might even be contemplating an apology.

But, no, she raised her brows as she asked, 'So, for the record, is this your right foot we're on now?'

He had to take a very deep breath to stop himself growling a response. She really was the most exasperating girl.

'Is everything a joke to you?' he muttered at length.

'Pretty much,' she admitted, 'but I can see you treat life seriously.'

Tiree pulled a long face in imitation of his and wondered how old Kit's stepfather was—forty going on seventy?

Sinclair's expression remained grave as he reminded her, 'You couldn't have found a great deal to laugh about over the last week or two.'

'Possibly not,' she agreed, 'but if you're hoping to see me crack up, you've got the wrong girl. I've been through harder times.'

'Really? I'm intrigued.' Sinclair half meant it, curious as to what had made this girl the way she was.

But she just cast him a disparaging glance, muttering, 'If I wanted to tell sob stories, I'd hire an analyst.'

'That can be arranged.' Sinclair genuinely wondered if her tough exterior might be a façade. 'If you asked Bob, I'm sure he'd—'

'Bob?' she picked out.

'Dr Chivers.'

'A friend is he?'

She was quick. Sinclair had to give her that.

'A colleague,' he amended.

'Well, *Bob* seemed quite happy with my current state of

health,' she relayed smugly. 'In fact, *Bob* has given me the all-clear to go home, no strait-jacket required.'

Sinclair seethed silently, unused to such opposition. He stared hard at the face upturned to his. It was quite perfect in feature and surprisingly young without make-up, but insolence curved the full lips and the green eyes seemed knowing rather than innocent.

He abandoned the idea of achieving any kind of civilised rapport and settled for making life difficult for her.

'Bob has agreed you may be discharged *under supervision*,' he stressed, 'so you'll need someone to take responsibility for you.'

Was he volunteering? Tiree could scarcely believe that. Their antipathy was mutual.

'Your parents, for instance,' he added.

'Unavailable.'

'What?'

'I have no parents,' Tiree admitted with a dare-to-pity-me glare.

Was she lying? 'You must have some other close relatives.'

'Must I?' she challenged, then, in mock-tragic tones, announced, 'No, it's just me. Poor little orphan Annie, all alone in the world.'

Sinclair understood she wasn't looking for sympathy which was fortunate because he felt no inclination to give any.

'Friends, then?' he persisted.

Tiree had them, of course, both in the world of pop and outside, but no one she fancied dragging into this. In fact, all she wanted was to get home, climb into bed, pull the covers over her head and sleep for a week.

But he was waiting for her to come up with someone so she suggested, 'My manager, Leslie Gray. Satisfied?'

'And you'll be able to stay at hers?'

'*His*. L-E-S-L-I-E. He'll come and stay with me.'

'I see,' he replied a little stiffly.

'I doubt it,' she muttered back.

'You're close?'

'Not especially, he lives in London.'

'I meant—'

'I know.'

Tiree raised defiant eyes to his, telling him to mind his own business.

Sinclair met her stare without apology, and proceeded to study her as if she were some new species to him.

Tiree waited for him to look away first. Normally people did. Not this man. His eyes were now the chilly blue of a winter sky yet she felt herself becoming warm all over.

She yielded first and hid the fact by wheeling herself back towards the telephone receiver on the nightstand. 'How do I dial out on this thing?'

'Nine,' he told her succinctly.

Tiree dialled it, then her manager's mobile number. She wasn't surprised when, after a couple of rings, she was put through to voicemail.

'Les, darling, it's Tiree. I need you to stay with me for a few days. *All* will be revealed, I promise, when you arrive.' She gave what she hoped passed for a sexy laugh and blew a couple of kisses down the telephone before hanging up.

She wondered what Les would make of the message, but she needn't worry that he'd get the wrong idea. Les preferred leggy blondes, the younger the better.

The point was to give her audience the wrong idea and from his glowering look, she succeeded.

'I take it Les *darling*,' his mouth twisted slightly, 'isn't likely to refuse such an invitation.'

'Would you?' Tiree pouted back without thinking.

An answer wasn't expected but it came with insulting haste, 'In a word, yes. As attractive as you may be, Miss Nemo, being a groupie has no appeal for me.'

His tone was dry rather than insulting, so Tiree didn't take particular offence. She could have told him groupies weren't her thing, anyway, but decided a subject change was wiser.

'Taxi firms,' she said instead, 'do you know any numbers?'

He shook his head. 'I'll drive you back to your cottage.'

The offer was as unexpected as it was unwelcome. 'I'd be quite happy with a taxi.'

'I wouldn't,' he countered. 'I intend to wait at the cottage until your manager turns up.'

His tone told her the matter wasn't up for discussion. Tiree wondered if he was following his own agenda or official hospital policy, as he walked round to grip the handles of her wheelchair.

She decided not to argue. She was too tired, anyway. Talking with this man was a very draining process.

Her only protest was a muttered, 'I *can* walk.'

'If you want to milk the sympathy vote,' he drawled back, 'then I suppose you could.'

That finally shut Tiree up. She hated any suggestion that she was inviting pity.

She allowed herself to be ushered from the room and along the corridor to a lift. They descended in silence and emerged into a reception area.

There was a girl manning the desk and several nurses hovering, dressed for going home but clearly in no hurry.

All eyes turned in Tiree's direction and she realised that her identity was no longer a secret.

She didn't flatter herself, however. She could discern disdain from admiration, and this was definitely not a fan club—more a stare at the wacko pop star committee.

To her relief, Sinclair barely hesitated but cut a swathe through the gawpers as if he owned the place. Maybe he did. Or had shares, anyway.

He pushed her out into the car park right to the door of an executive saloon car. It was just the kind of car she could have predicted he'd own—discreet model, conservative colour, comfort before ostentation.

'Thanks.' The expression of gratitude slipped out.

He looked surprised as if he might ask, 'For what?' but confined himself to saying, 'Do you need a hand to get in?'

She shook her head and used her arms to lever herself out of the chair. The ankle still hurt but she managed to bear her weight on it. He held the door open and she manoeuvred herself into the car.

While he disposed of the chair, she sank back in the leather and shut her eyes. Perhaps if she kept them closed, she could discourage conversation until they got to the door of her cottage.

She was aware of Sinclair climbing into the driver's seat and starting the engine. He put the car in gear and drove off but they didn't get very far before he suddenly applied the brakes.

Tiree sat up, alert, and saw they'd stopped short of the gates at the bottom of the drive. She saw the reason, too. A crowd of people were milling about on the other side.

'Reporters, I take it,' Sinclair voiced her fears aloud.

Was that an accusation? 'Don't look at me!'

He continued to do so, however, his eyes boring into hers as he said, 'Someone must have rung them up.'

'Yeah,' Tiree rolled her eyes, 'like I'd give the Daily Trash a call and say come take a photo of me, straight out of hospital and looking like this.'

He pursed his lips—before revving his engine to catch the attention of the security guard manning the small gatehouse.

The Pack had already noticed them and some were clambering on the gates when Sinclair indicated to the porter to open up. On a remote, the gates inched apart with exasperating slowness.

Sinclair bided his time until they were fully open, then made a controlled run at the gap, forcing the journalists to fall back.

Tiree was conscious of the flashing bulbs and the rapping of hands on the car roof but she sat stiff as a board and eyes front. She knew from experience that if she covered her face or ducked down, the photographs would look so much worse— as if she was distraught or ashamed or running scared.

Sinclair would have liked to accelerate away but, with visions of the headline, DOCTOR'S DEADLY DRIVE, he slowed to make a right turn out onto the main road.

Knuckles were now drumming on the window glass, trying to gain his attention, cameras shoved in front of his windshield, hands pulling at the doors which he'd had the presence of mind to lock.

It couldn't have been for more than twenty seconds but it

felt like an assault by a pack of wild animals before he was finally able to pull out onto the road and speed away.

It left him tense with anger and wanting to lash out. 'Get a nice shot, did they?'

Tiree understood the nature of the accusation but didn't respond. She was shaking inside. If she'd ever liked the Press attention—and she couldn't remember a time she really had—it was now an anathema to her.

'You didn't exactly bother hiding, did you?' he added, just in case she failed to take his meaning.

'And let them see me cowering like an animal?' she hissed back. 'Well, sod that.'

Sweet and kind and funny. That had been his stepson Kit's one-time description of her. He hadn't believed it then and it seemed pitifully misguided now.

'Still, they got a good one of you,' she had to point out, 'snarling into their cameras.'

'What are you saying?' he demanded. 'That I should have smiled nicely and given them a wave?'

'You should have done nothing,' Tiree advised somewhat late. 'Chances are they wouldn't even have recognised me... You have seen my professional appearance, haven't you?'

'The blonde tart-look, yes,' he confirmed.

Tiree flinched a little at the description but then decided to let it pass. She appreciated the real source of his anger. He'd clearly hated the Press attention. Well, that gave them one thing in common, at least.

At her failure to respond, Sinclair glanced from the road and saw her staring sightlessly ahead. It was then he remembered he was supposed to be a doctor, and that insulting a recently discharged patient wasn't quite in the spirit of the Hippocratic oath.

'Look, I'm sorry.'

'For what?'

'My last remark.' It didn't seem wise to repeat it.

But she just shrugged. 'As you sow, so shall you reap.'

Sinclair did a double-take, both at the sentiment and the fact she was quoting the bible at him. He supposed it made a change from her earlier 'sod off' but it was hardly what he'd expected of Miss Ti Nemo, rock chick.

So what *had* he expected? He'd seen her once on television, wild blonde hair, black leather mini and slashed top, but he hadn't taken much notice; he'd been more interested in Kit playing guitar in the background. She'd looked much the same yesterday in court, clothes toned down somewhat, but still the blonde wig and make-up applied with a trowel, and she'd almost been monosyllabic, offering the briefest of answers to the coroner. Fundamentally stupid he'd decided then. How wrong could a person be?

Sinclair wondered now what was image and what was real. 'That's not your proper name, is it? Ti Nemo?'

Tiree dragged her mind back from elsewhere, laughing shortly, 'Would I make something like that up?'

Sinclair thought it possible. 'Most pop stars' names seem outlandish to me these days.'

Tiree conceded he had a point but did he have to sound so stuffy making it. 'How old are you?'

'How old?' he echoed. 'Why?'

'Just curious,' she replied, 'since we're trading personal questions.'

Sinclair's lips compressed even as he said, 'Thirty-eight,' rather than seem coy about it.

'*Really*?' Tiree affected surprise.

Sinclair's mouth was now a thin, tight line. How old did the damn girl think he was, fifty? He'd always imagined he looked his age, no more or less.

Tiree sensed she'd touched a nerve but didn't care. He may not look it, but boy, did he act old.

'So *is* it your name?'

'It is now, yes.'

'You changed it by deed poll,' he concluded.

Tiree shook her head. 'The Ti is short for Tiree, an island in Scotland.'

'Yes, I know it.'

'I was brought up in a commune near there.'

'A commune?' Another unlikely story. 'And the Nemo?'

'The commune chose that part, too. Apparently it means "no one".'

'In Latin, yes.'

Trust him to be up on a dead language. 'Which seemed appropriate, seeing as I was left on their doorstep at a few hours old.'

Sinclair didn't hide his incredulity now. 'You're saying you were a foundling?'

Tiree wrinkled her nose at the term. It sounded Dickensian. He'd be asking next if she'd been born in a workhouse. Well, what had she been expecting from him? Sensitivity?

She wished now she'd stuck to the official fan-club version of her childhood: death of single mother leading to teenage years in the care of a Glasgow corporation and a spell of homelessness before fame and fortune beckoned. It approximated the truth without betraying a more outlandish reality.

'You made that up, didn't you?' he accused at her silence.

Tiree questioned why she'd confided in him in the first place. 'Possibly.'

Sinclair took this as a yes. 'The same as you did your name, I presume.'

'Does it matter?' Tiree didn't see it did. 'A rose would smell as sweet, and all that.'

Now she was quoting Shakespeare at him. Was there no end to this girl's talents?

'Did the band write its own songs?' he suddenly thought of asking.

Tiree blinked at this apparent *non sequitur* before relaying, 'Stu penned most of the hits, but Kit and I did a couple together for the new album... Was he really your stepson?'

He answered by saying, 'I don't tell lies.'

Unlike her—was that the implication? Well, he was right, she supposed. Lying, she'd discovered, had often served her better than the truth.

'Kit never mentioned you,' she stated flatly.

'He mentioned you,' Sinclair countered with an edge.

Tiree frowned. Had Kit said bad things about her? She doubted it.

'And?' she prompted.

'And nothing.' Sinclair chose to keep Kit's opinions to himself rather than tell this girl how much Kit had been under her spell.

Tiree decided not to pursue it, either. They were nearly at the cottage. Ten minutes and she'd be home. If he insisted on waiting until Les arrived, then that was up to him. She'd go and seek sanctuary in her bedroom.

She went back to studying the scenery, and, when her eyes became heavy, leaned her head against the window and allowed herself to slip into a doze.

Sinclair didn't require directions. He'd been to her cottage before last night. Kit had given him the address as a contact and, two days after his death, Sinclair had searched the country lanes outside Windsor for Ivy Cottage. On finding it, he'd banged on the door until his knuckles hurt and he was forced to accept Miss Nemo was not currently in residence.

He'd wanted the same thing then—some kind of explanation as to what had happened that night to cause his stepson to be so careless with his life. Now he considered a change of tactics. Perhaps if he adopted a more neutral tone, they might manage a reasonable conversation before the manager appeared.

Sinclair wondered what he'd be like, *darling* Les. A definite suggestion of intimacy there, but did that mean anything? She'd probably been to bed with half the men she'd met, Kit included.

He glanced at her in profile. If she suffered at all from conscience, it didn't show. She slept serenely, long lashes shadowing a pale but flawless complexion. Which girl had Kit imagined he loved—the rampant blonde rock star or this green-eyed creature whose face reflected an innocence that just had to be a lie?

Kit had always had a kind heart, Sinclair reflected. He remembered the first time he'd met him, a shy little boy of five. He'd taken to him instantly, although it wouldn't have mattered if he hadn't. He'd been so madly in love with Nicole he'd have married her, regardless.

Hard to believe how blind he'd been. The marriage had been

doomed from the start. They'd been too different although arguably that's why they'd been attracted to each other. Having been through one turbulent relationship, Nicole had been looking for calm, strong and rational, while he had been drawn to her sheer vivacity.

But love hadn't survived the reality. A year or two of playing mother and doctor's wife, Nicole was restless and looking for excitement. He was just weary, trying to reconcile himself to an endless round of parties and her habit of provoking arguments for a reaction. Working long hours, he had felt guilty enough to trust her burgeoning friendship with Jack Andrews, the financier. But, in his heart, he had probably known.

When she'd run away, there had been as much relief as anger. Part of him accepted parting as inevitable, and his primary concern had been for Kit whom Nicole had failed to take with her. Fortunately he'd grown fond of his, by then, seven-year-old stepson, and it had suited him well enough.

Four months had gone by before Nicole reappeared, contrite and begging for a reconciliation. He must have been mad to agree, but, with Kit to consider and a memory still of once loving her, he'd allowed her a second chance to humiliate him.

Of course it hadn't worked. Nothing had changed. He was still a hard-working junior doctor and she was still the party lover. That time the parting had been even bloodier, an acrimonious split that had involved lawyers and custody cases. He'd lost Kit, a fact he might have tolerated better if Nicole hadn't immediately abandoned the boy to her elderly parents and thence, to the boarding school system.

All contact was severed and Nicole had moved onto more exciting orbits. She'd been with a rally driver at the time of her death. A man who'd liked speed off the race track as well as on, he'd hurtled them off a cliff near Nice.

It seemed years ago but in fact it was only three. That's when he'd re-entered Kit's life.

He'd been happy to do so, but he quickly realised it wasn't a case of picking up things where they were left off. The Kit he'd known was a boy who liked to go fishing, build plastic models of motorbikes and watch Star Wars videos back to back. The new Kit was an uncommunicative teenager, a quiet rebel whose only interest was music and his guitar.

He had tried. They had both tried. But it was no use. Too late. Past the time when Kit might have welcomed a father-figure to keep him straight. Sinclair had tried reading the Riot Act a few times. Kit had done the courtesy of listening—he was always a polite child—but it had failed to make an impact. Kit had left school the moment he could.

Sinclair had been powerless to stop him so he'd settled for keeping in touch, however sporadically. Kit would turn up on his doorstep, broke and hungry, and he'd feed and house him for a couple of weeks before the boy would disappear back to London.

Asked about his plans, Kit always said he wanted to be a musician. His stepfather had been sceptical, although he knew Kit could play quite well. When Kit had actually ended up in a band, he'd tried to be pleased for him, but it soon became evident that the rock lifestyle was no myth and he'd been forced to watch on the sidelines as Kit lost his way in the prevailing drug culture.

He hadn't needed to perform a blood test to know Kit was on something during his last visit. He'd done his stint in ca-sualty, recognised the behaviour pattern and the edgy laughter. Nor had he to meet Ti Nemo, the band's singer, to be con-vinced she'd had a part in his downfall.

Had Kit been taken in by her apparent vulnerability? That idiotic tale of being left on a doorstep? It seemed likely. For all his difficult childhood, Kit had never been very worldly. Sinclair imagined Ti Nemo would have run rings round him.

Determined she wouldn't do the same to him, Sinclair finally nudged her awake on the home stretch.

Murmuring a protest, Tiree blinked her eyes open and saw they were nearly at her cottage.

It was situated in quite a rural location on a B road between two bends. Tiree had bought it for this isolation, needing a bolt-hole from the manic, rock and roll lifestyle.

'Just up here on the left,' she instructed, forgetting he'd been there last night.

Sinclair began to slow down, ready to pull in, when he saw not one but three cars parked rather precariously on the verge. He was quick to react, his foot back on the accelerator to speed on past.

'Hey, you've…' Tiree started to protest before she, too, realised the significance of the vehicles. 'Press? No, it can't be,' she added, craning her neck to catch sight of a photographer, camera slung round his neck.

'It certainly looks like it,' Sinclair drawled before travelling on for half a mile and parking in a field entrance.

Tiree slumped back in the passenger seat. Who had told them? She had always assumed few people knew of her cottage, yet the man beside her had found it and, up until yesterday, she hadn't even been aware of *his* existence.

'How did you know where my cottage was?' she asked him now.

'When Kit moved out of his London flat,' he relayed, 'he sent us a forwarding address—yours.'

Us? Tiree observed the use of the collective pronoun and assumed there must be a second wife, perhaps currently waiting for him to return home.

'I didn't tell anyone if that's what you're driving at,' he continued with an edge.

'If you say so.' Tiree was less than convinced.

He turned in the driver's seat to give her one of his superior looks. 'Do you actually believe I'd want my name and reputation linked with yours? I'm a paediatric consultant, not some bimbo-chasing footballer with brains in my feet.'

Tiree bristled at the bimbo and the sheer intellectual snobbery of it.

'Well, don't worry,' she sniped back, 'I don't imagine anyone would seriously consider I'd date someone like you, either.'

'Good!' Sinclair disregarded the implicit insult. 'So, what do you suggest we do now?'

We? Another collective, him and her this time. It surprised her. No need for him to do anything other than set her down beside the road and let her walk back and face the music alone.

But then he still wanted something from her: an account of events on the night Stu and Kit had crashed.

She could easily give it. She could relay chapter and verse until he wished he'd never asked, but she was bound by loyalties that surely extended beyond death.

'If you want me to drive back to the cottage,' Sinclair declared, 'I'll do so.'

Tiree shook her head. She couldn't face another rugby scrum like yesterday, being jostled and hectored by a pack of pressmen on the courtroom steps.

Les and the band solicitor had managed to extricate her but some of the paparazzi had followed, weaving through traffic on their motorbikes, pursuing them to Les's offices from where she'd called a black cab to spirit her away via the rear exit.

She'd changed into nondescript clothes and discarded her wig, confident of being another anonymous punter to the cabbie. He certainly hadn't given any indication that he'd rumbled who she was, although, on reflection, she had caught him eyeballing her in his rear-view mirror a few times. Maybe he *had* recognised her and alerted the Press.

Not that it mattered who had betrayed her whereabouts. It was done. Her cottage was no longer a sanctuary. All she wanted now was to walk away from it.

'Would you drive me to the nearest station?' she asked of Sinclair, adding tactfully, 'Please.'

She'd obviously abandoned plans to go home and Sinclair wasn't about to persuade her otherwise, but he still asked, 'Where do you intend going?'

'I don't know,' Tiree admitted. 'London, probably. I could book into a hotel.'

Sinclair glanced her way. 'Have you any money?'

'Of course I have money.' The band had had six consecutive charting singles. 'Just not on me… I thought you could loan me some.'

'Did you now?' he reflected unhelpfully.

She held in a sigh of irritation. 'Do you want me to beg?'

'Would you?' He raised a mocking brow.

She awarded him a look far from supplication, before snapping, 'No!'

'We seem to have reached an impasse, then.' Sinclair supposed he meant to bait her as he put the car back in gear.

But he didn't expect her to suddenly unclick her seat belt and push open the passenger door, saying, 'I'm not going back there.'

'Wait up!' He made a grab for her but she was too quick, swinging her legs out onto the verge.

Tiree had forgotten her bad ankle but was reminded as she hit the ground. She ignored the pain, however, to walk in the direction that took her away from the cottage.

Sinclair watched in disbelief as she limped along the verge. No hat, no coat and no purse. Just the plain white T-shirt and jeans she'd been wearing the night before. And though it was early summer, a drizzling rain had begun to fall.

Perhaps she was crazy and the wisest thing was to let her go. So why grab an overcoat and follow in hot pursuit?

Sinclair didn't have an answer.

Tiree didn't spare him a glance, as he drew level, but hissed at him, 'Go away!'

'This is ridiculous.' He put out a hand to stop her.

She shrugged it off and repeated, 'Then go away!'

But he kept pace with her, pointing out, 'You're getting wet and your ankle must be hurting.'

'So?' Tiree's temper was keeping her warm and oblivious of pain.

'Come on, Ti—' he used her name for the first time '—let's go back to the car.'

It made her slow and finally glance in his direction.

He was wearing his 'let's humour the idiot' face which Tiree recognised from earlier. She awarded him a venomous look in reply and, when he tried to drape an overcoat round her, she chucked it off and kept walking.

Or would have if a hand hadn't clamped on her arm, bringing her up short.

This time, when she tried to shake him loose, he held tight and she ended up hurting herself.

'Let me go!' she spat in his direction.

He ignored it, saying, 'We're going back to the car.'

'You'll have to carry me first,' she retorted, digging her heels in.

'Right.' Sinclair decided to take her literally.

Without her high-heel boots, her 'big' hair and her leather gear, Tiree was a very slight figure, five feet four and slim built. No problem to a man almost a head taller and with a fairly muscular physique.

He draped the overcoat round her first, muttering, 'Hold on to me!'

Then he bent an arm round her shoulders and knees to lift her clean off her feet.

At first Tiree obeyed out of sheer shock, before acquiescence became mandatory as he strode back along the verge, forcing her to lace her fingers round his neck while her head bobbed against the wall of his chest. The drizzle was fast turning into a downpour and he seemed to gather her closer, as if to cocoon her from the worst of the elements.

When he finally reached the passenger door, Tiree was overwhelmed by a rare sense of helplessness. Unusual in itself, it had all kinds of side affects. Dizzy head, racing heart and a body heat that defied the cold rain.

Sinclair was contending with some fairly mixed emotions, too. He didn't like this girl. She wasn't his type, physically, mentally or morally. But none of these factors stopped his body reacting to her proximity.

He carefully lowered her to the ground and she looked up at him with those wide, green eyes of hers. He held her a little longer, noticing, for the first time it seemed, a face so naturally beautiful it made him forget all the other things about her and obey his baser instincts.

Tiree could have turned away. She had the chance. Five, maybe ten seconds, passed between his gaze shifting to her mouth and his mouth inching towards hers. She actually had the thought: he's going to kiss me. Dismissed it as crazy even as his mouth lowered to hers.

She even had the time to wonder: Why am I doing this? Not

sufficient to find an answer, however, before they were actually doing it.

And who would have thought it, the man would kiss like that? A whisper against her mouth slowly became a caress, so gentle it quelled panic, stirred desire, before his lips finally hardened, opened to possess and carry her along on the tide.

She tried to keep her head out of water, but it was swimming round and round, and she was drowning and still the kiss went on and on, demanding a response from her until she was trembling from the sheer force of it.

She grabbed at a lifeline, but it was just his shoulders and she was dragged back again, hauled against his hard body.

She gasped for breath and he gave her his own, groaning into her mouth as he deepened the kiss until it was an intimate clash of lips and teeth and tongue.

Sinclair had lost sight of who she was, who he was, forgotten Kit, cold in his grave and needing retribution. He'd even forgotten the rain. Only when he sought to touch her skin and discovered her wet through did sanity return.

Then he finally asked himself, What am I doing? but didn't attempt an answer, before pulling away in angry frustration.

CHAPTER FOUR

HE RELEASED her so abruptly Tiree fell back against the car. Her eyes sought his and she saw her own confusion reflected back at her. Then he unlocked the car and almost pushed her into the passenger seat.

She sat where she'd been put, shaken and shivering. She felt she'd stepped into a bad film where a fantasy sequence had suddenly been introduced. No explanation for it or the resumption of normality.

Better if it had been a film. She might have known her lines. Instead she was on her own, stuck for any response as he climbed into the scat beside her.

Tiree considered outrage as a possible reaction but it wasn't really her style. Anyway, she was a bit late: the time for slapping his face was *before* he kissed her not *after* she'd enjoyed it.

And she had. That was the real mind-blower. The fact that for once she'd felt all the corny emotions written about in love stories—heart racing, head spinning, earth moving—for a man she'd disliked on sight.

He glanced briefly in her direction, but mercifully made no comment as he swivelled round to rummage in a sports bag on the back seat.

'Here.' A towel was dropped in her lap, followed by a man's polo shirt. 'Get out of your wet top, at least.'

Tiree's face conveyed her feelings. Did he imagine one kiss and she was ready to strip off in front of him? She wasn't even wearing a bra.

Sinclair read her expression and his lips pursed, realising she now had him written down as a sex maniac. Rather than debate the point, he opened his door, muttering, 'I'll give you a couple of minutes.'

Thankfully it had stopped raining and Tiree watched as he

climbed back out of the car and walked a couple of yards away, then stood, hands in pockets, facing away from her.

She was tempted to defy him and remain in her wet T-shirt, but it was clammy and uncomfortable and she couldn't seem to stop shivering although it was mid-May. She made the decision and pulled the wet material off as quickly as possible, rubbed herself with the towel, then dressed in his polo shirt, having placed her discarded top into a side pocket in the door.

His garment drowned her, of course, and, although it was clean, it still managed to smell of him. She wondered how she was going to get a change of clothes without suffering the attentions of the Press who were camped out at the cottage. She glared at Sinclair's back, somehow feeling it was all his fault even if logic said otherwise, and left him to stand there another thirty seconds before blowing the horn to permit his return.

Once back in the car, he announced rather stiffly, 'I shouldn't have kissed you.'

If it was meant as an apology, Tiree was unimpressed: zero contrition in the tone and the word sorry didn't figure at all. Instead he was wearing that superior look of his—the 'I'm a terribly clever doctor and therefore right about everything' expression.

'No, you shouldn't,' she agreed stonily and returned to staring out of the side window.

A silence followed while Sinclair wondered what she expected. He'd apologised, hadn't he? And he wasn't even sure if the kiss was entirely his fault.

'Perhaps if you weren't so provocative,' he found himself suggesting.

'*Provocative*?' Tiree's disbelief was genuine. 'What—in jeans and T-shirt?'

A wet T-shirt and no bra, Sinclair could have rejoined, but that would be to admit how much he'd noticed—and undermine his attempt to recover some dignity.

'I was referring to the way you speak,' he responded, 'your somewhat confrontational manner.'

On the point of arguing back—and thus proving his point—

Tiree counted slowly to ten before muttering under her breath, 'Better than being pompous, anyway.'

Sinclair caught it, as intended, and was surprised by how much he minded. Perhaps because there was some truth in it.

He resisted the urge to trade insults and, switching on the engine, put the car into reverse gear.

'I'm not going back to the cottage,' Tiree repeated her earlier statement.

'That isn't my intention,' Sinclair dismissed, 'a fact I would have conveyed earlier, had I been given the chance.'

Pompous, pompous, pompous, Tiree confirmed her original diagnosis but limited herself to face-pulling this time.

'Trust me, I have no wish to feature as your *mystery companion* in some tabloid newspaper... How is your ankle, by the way?' he added, switching to doctor mode.

The brief walk had left it throbbing slightly but Tiree just shrugged. 'It's fine.'

'You need to rest it,' he advised before pulling back onto the main carriageway.

Tiree nodded vaguely, more concerned about his next move, but he was as good as his word, driving past her cottage without slowing down.

Tiree glanced towards her home and remarked aloud, 'There was a car in the actual drive. It looked like my manager's.'

A sports model, there couldn't be many custom-painted that bilious green.

'He couldn't have received your message and driven down from London by now,' Sinclair queried the timescales.

'He could already have been on his way.' Tiree knew her manager was anxious to capitalise on her recent front-page coverage.

'The Press may have alerted him about your accident,' Sinclair surmised.

'I suppose.' Tiree wondered who had tipped off the Press.

The same question was occupying Sinclair's mind. 'Or maybe it was vice versa and your manager alerted the Press?'

'Les?' she echoed. 'But how would he have known?'

'Has he a key to your cottage?' Sinclair's enquiry drew a

nod. 'I left a "to whom it may concern" note, after I put a makeshift board against the broken window.'

'I broke a window?' Tiree had no recollection of that.

'No, *I* did,' Sinclair amended, 'in order to get in. You can bill me for repair if you wish.'

'Yeah, that would make a great headline,' Tiree scoffed, 'SINGER STINGY TO SUAVE SURGEON SAVIOUR.'

Sinclair cringed at the alliteration although it was close to what the most down-market tabloids might write.

'How about we forget the window and the saviour nonsense,' he suggested, 'and both agree to keep quiet about the whole incident?'

'Yeah, okay.' Tiree had no problem with that—well, apart from his obvious loathing to be associated with her. 'But, for the record, why did you help me?'

He'd obviously arrived at the cottage and realised she was hurt. He could have walked away at that point. They both knew that.

'Because I'm a doctor.' Plain statement of fact. He'd obeyed ingrained instincts.

Tiree pulled a slight face. 'I imagine your usual patients are more effusive.'

An acknowledgement of her own lack of gratitude, she was surprised by the sharpness of his response.

'Let's get one thing straight,' he almost barked at her, 'you are not my patient.'

The point was underlined by a glare. Tiree wondered what she'd said to cause such a reaction.

Enlightenment slowly dawned. Doctors weren't allowed to go round kissing their patients, were they? Therefore she mustn't be his patient.

Well, she wasn't about to try and make trouble for him.

'That's okay by me. I prefer my doctors sympathetic.'

'Or obliging?'

Tiree understood the implication. Stu had had an obliging doctor, a provider of uppers and downers on request.

'I don't do drugs,' she stated categorically.

Sinclair glanced from the road again and caught a look of injured innocence. What an actress!

'If you say so.' He didn't hide his scepticism.

'Oh, think what you like!' Tiree was used to people's assumption that rock singer equated with dope-head. 'Your opinion scarcely matters. As you say, you're not my doctor.'

'Nor ever likely to be,' he added, 'considering I'm a paediatrician. And, actually, children don't tend to be particularly effusive. Sick, they're too miserable. Well again, and they can't wait to leave.'

His dry tone suggested he liked things this way. Perhaps children didn't notice his lack of bedside manner.

'I imagine their parents are all over you, though,' surmised Tiree.

'Sometimes,' he admitted, 'but nothing on the scale of adulation you must receive as a rock superstar.'

Tiree supposed she deserved that for implying he was in medicine for the ego-stroking.

'I'd hardly term myself a superstar,' she refuted, 'and if you think that kind of adulation is enjoyable, you're crazier than the several crazies who have stalked me during the last couple of years.'

'You're exaggerating?'

'I wish. Why do you think I went into panic mode when you called? My last admirer camped outside my London flat for two days, then started to kick the door down when he finally realised I wasn't going to invite him in for tea. By the time the police showed up, he was inside and making serious headway on the bathroom door where I'd locked myself in.'

She relayed this story in her usual, tough, seen-it-all manner, but Sinclair understood the incident must have shaken her. Hence last night's pre-emptive threat to call the police.

'Did the whole band have obsessed fans or just you?' he asked her.

'I don't think Kit or Wayne did,' she recalled, 'but Stu had a few.'

'Stuart Maclennan, the driver of the car?' he echoed.

She nodded, figuring he'd heard Stu's full name from the coroner's court.

No doubt Stu was on his hate list, too. The police report favoured the scenario where Kit had overtaken Stu on a dangerous bend before losing control of his motorbike, causing them both to crash, but with the amphetamines found in Stu's body, some saw him as the villain.

'Why Maclennan and not the other two males in the band?' Sinclair pursued.

'Stu had the most charisma,' Tiree supposed. 'He also wrote the lyrics to our songs. That was probably a factor… Have you listened to any?'

'Not sufficiently to decipher the words.'

'Well, they tend to be on the deep and depressing side, which led some fans to believe Stu alone could relate to their angst.'

'Not just fans,' countered Sinclair. 'Kit called Maclennan brilliant and insightful, too. In fact, he was in awe of both of you, at least in the beginning before things started to unravel for him.'

A purposeful note had crept into his voice and reminded Tiree just why this man had entered her life. He wanted to know the circumstances that had led up to the accident.

She refused to comment.

'You were involved with him, weren't you?' he added abruptly.

Tiree was unsure to which 'him' he referred. 'You mean Kit?'

Sinclair took it as stalling tactics rather than a denial. 'Who else might I mean?'

'I don't know.'

'Maclennan? You had a history with him, too, didn't you?'

Yes, Tiree had a history with Stu. She had loved him, in fact. But this man would never understand.

He proved it as he ran on, 'Was that what was going on— a *ménage à trois*, only one of you wanted it to be *à deux*?'

Tiree might have worked up more indignation if a couple of the tabloids hadn't already hinted the same.

'Well?' Sinclair read her silence as guilt.

But no, she was merely weary. 'You don't expect me to dignify that question with an answer, do you?'

'Yes,' he grated out, 'if you don't want me to do a U-turn back to your cottage.'

Empty threat? Possibly. They were already miles away. But his expression was serious enough.

'I liked Kit,' she replied at length, 'I liked him a great deal. But not the way you're implying. He was just a kid as far as I was concerned.'

Sinclair might have believed her, aware she was twenty-three to Kit's nineteen and seeming even older, but sensed she was hiding something.

She'd returned to staring out of the window, asking, 'Where exactly are we going?'

Till that point Sinclair hadn't made up his mind.

'My house isn't far,' he found himself saying. 'You can stay there tonight until you make alternative arrangements.'

'Yeah, right.' Tiree's tone accused him of ulterior motives.

An hour ago, Sinclair could have claimed with absolute conviction that she had no need to worry—he'd sooner go to bed with a good book than a bad girl like her. Of course, that was before he'd succumbed to a moment's madness and kissed her, an action now as embarrassing as it was inexplicable.

'I can provide a chaperone,' he ran on. 'My housekeeper lives in the nearest village and stays on occasion.'

He was back in his comfort zone, sounding stiff and pompous and leading Tiree to judge that any man who suggested a chaperone had to be living in another century and, consequently, be safe enough. 'I'll go with the Mrs Mop plan as long as she isn't going to blab to the newspapers.'

'Mrs *Enderby*,' he stressed the name, 'is, I assure you, completely trustworthy. Otherwise I would hardly risk making *myself* an object of salacious tabloid journalism, would I?'

His tone said not. He clearly considered himself above all that. A respectable doctor with no desire to be tainted by the dubious world in which she operated.

Yet he had tried it on with her, hadn't he? Just like a long line of rejects before him. A niggling voice reminded her she hadn't exactly rejected *his* advances, but she'd been getting round to it.

She wondered if it had been a test to see how easy she was. One she suspected she'd failed. Well, she wouldn't if it was repeated. He'd soon discover she was no pushover.

Another five minutes and they'd arrived at one of those essentially English villages with ivy-covered cottages, a quaint pub called the Coach and Horses and an ancient church with surrounding graveyard. He turned off at the latter, onto a track that wound up a hill and petered out after a few hundred yards at a house called the Old Vicarage.

Half-hidden by a high brick wall, it wasn't until they'd driven through automatic gates that Tiree appreciated the size of the double-fronted Victorian house, built for a clergyman and requisite large family.

'This is your house?' She didn't hide her surprise.

He nodded. 'What did you expect?'

Tiree wasn't sure, but remarked rather bluntly, 'They must pay consultants fairly well.'

'Not as well as footballers or pop stars,' he countered drily, 'and if you're wondering how I could afford it, the answer is I couldn't. I inherited it from my parents.'

Well, he was honest, Tiree conceded, but trust him to come from money.

He stepped out of the car, and walked round to open her door. 'Do you need any help?'

She shook her head. She was wary of him touching her, even if it was just a supporting hand on her elbow.

Fortunately he didn't insist, but led the way to the front door, leaving her to follow at a slower, limping pace.

He unlocked the door and went inside, triggering off the alarm warning. Tiree lingered on the doorstep, considering a bid for freedom. She could go into the village and hope to order a taxi, although it might be somewhat difficult hampered by a painful ankle and no money.

'Are you coming in?' Sinclair had returned to the doorstep to find her mid-debate.

He sounded more impatient than anything. Certainly not a

man bent on seduction. In fact, he talked to her in a manner reassuring in its indifference.

Tiree took a couple of steps over the threshold, entering a dark hall of panelled oak. She had time to look round while he sorted through his mail, discarding most of it back onto an umbrella stand.

'I'm going to telephone my housekeeper,' he informed her. 'The kitchen is at the end of the hall if you want a drink.'

He nodded towards a corridor leading to the back of the house and didn't wait for a response before disappearing into another room. He left the door ajar and Tiree glimpsed shelves groaning with the weight of hardback books in a library study.

She hovered for a moment, then hearing him pick up the phone, wandered off to the kitchen.

After all, was she in any real danger from this man? If he'd wanted to punish her for Kit, he'd had his chance last night. He wouldn't have had to do anything, just leave her unconscious at the foot of the stairs.

She entered the kitchen and stood for a moment, taking in her surroundings. It was a light, airy room, with windows which faced south, and very clean and tidy, no dirty dishes in the sink or clutter on surfaces, but the dark-oak units and built-in cooker suggested someone had last taken an interest in the decor circa early nineties.

It answered one question for Tiree: there was no current Mrs Sinclair.

She picked up the kettle and crossed to fill it at the sink, still nursing her ankle. She reached for the cold tap, then stopped mid-action, meeting a set of eyes staring at her through the window. She jumped and almost dropped the kettle before she had a good look at the stranger outside.

It was a child. A boy she thought at first, with short blonde hair, before she realised the face was too pretty. It did, however, bear a strong resemblance to a certain male, scowl and all.

The girl made a gesture towards the side and Tiree understood there must be an outer door further along.

The kitchen led into a utility room with stone sinks and a

back servants' staircase. There was also a heavy oak door. She had to slide various bolts and turn a key in the lock before it opened.

'Hello,' she greeted the girl with a smile.

It was not returned. The girl stood for a moment, giving her the once-over, before shrugging her way past.

Tiree followed her to the kitchen and had the question, 'Where's my father?' flung at her.

'In his study,' she replied evenly.

The next question was even ruder, a very direct, 'Who are you?'

Tiree considered how she was going to answer that one. Like Sinclair, she didn't want to advertise where she'd been on this 'lost' day.

'Just a friend,' she volunteered at length.

'You mean a *girlfriend*?' Sinclair's young daughter sneered back.

Tiree could have taken offence but she recognised this show of disdain for what it was: insecurity.

She tried to make a joke of it. 'Do I look like your dad's type?'

'Not much,' the girl agreed, still unsmiling, 'but that doesn't prove anything. Men of my dad's age often start dating younger and younger women.'

'Really!' Tiree wasn't going to argue with this authoritative statement.

'How old *are* you?' the girl added.

'Twenty-three.'

'Not that young, then.'

To a girl of her years, probably not, Tiree conceded.

'How old are *you*?' she countered.

'Thirteen…almost,' the girl admitted.

'Does your dad know you're here?' Tiree drew a shrug and wondered why Sinclair had failed to mention the existence of this child. 'Did you forget your key?'

The latter elicited a resentful, 'He won't give me one.'

Tiree frowned. Did Sinclair expect the child to hang around

outside till he arrived home? That was worse, surely, than her being a latch-key kid.

'Perhaps if you explained—' Tiree began to suggest, but was left talking to thin air as approaching footsteps sent the girl scuttling in the opposite direction.

Tiree guessed she was heading for the back staircase about the same time as Sinclair entered the kitchen.

She didn't get a chance to speak, before he ran on, 'There's a message on my answering machine, informing me my daughter's absconded from school. I have to go and look for her. Will you stay in case she turns up?'

'No need. She's here already.'

'Here?'

'I assume it's her. Blonde, tall, looks like you?'

A succession of emotions crossed his face, worry to relief then finally anger. 'You've seen her?'

'She was in the garden,' Tiree relayed, 'so I let her in. We chatted for a few moments, then she went upstairs to change.'

The last was definitely poetic licence. The girl had flown upstairs to avoid Sinclair and, presumably, his wrath.

It was partially directed at Tiree as he demanded, 'You didn't say who *you* were?'

'I told her I wasn't a girlfriend, if that's what's bothering you,' she stated shortly.

'She's hardly likely to think that.' A haughty look suggested Tiree would never pass the criterion.

'She did, actually,' Tiree took satisfaction in telling him. 'Seems to think you might be going through a mid-life crisis, *vis-à-vis* your dating habits.'

'What?'

'Younger women.'

'Right.' He scowled comprehension. 'Nonetheless, I'd prefer you did keep your identity from Eloise. She's still upset about her brother's death.'

'She's Kit's sister?'

'Half-sister. Same mother, different father.'

'You never said you had a child,' she remarked in slightly accusing tones.

'You never asked,' he countered, 'and I didn't imagine it would become relevant. In fact, it won't be as she will be returning to school forthwith.'

'Just like that?' Tiree wondered how he could make such an instant decision.

'As opposed to?'

'I imagine she's run away for a reason. Don't you think you should find it out first?'

A brow shot up at her presumption. 'Correct me if I'm wrong, but *you* don't have any children, do you?'

Meaning: so what right did she have to dispense advice?

Tiree, however, wasn't quelled. 'No, but I *was* once a teenage girl and I *have* run away.'

'And that makes you an expert?' Both brows were raised this time. 'Well, excuse me, if I don't canvass the opinion of a rock singer who probably sleeps—'

Sinclair broke off mid-sentence, deciding not to voice an accusation for which he had no proof.

He was too late, however. Tiree could fill in the blanks. Who sleeps with every man she meets? Something along those lines, she was willing to bet.

She shot him a hostile look, while conceding she might not be the ideal person to dispense advice.

But then again, maybe she was, her own life having gone so badly off the rails. She could certainly recognise crucial stages in her childhood when wrong decisions had been made, not always by her but the adult world.

'Anyway, I know why Eloise runs away,' he claimed, 'but hating school scarcely gives her the right, legal or otherwise, to abscond.'

Tiree picked up on the run*s* away. 'She's done it before?'

He nodded briefly before curtailing the subject with a clipped, 'Are you hungry?'

'A bit, yes.'

'Then help yourself,' he suggested, 'while I do my poor best to *reason* with my daughter.'

No reply was expected to this sarcasm as he turned on his heel and left the kitchen. Tiree was confined to making a face at his back. She heard his heavy footsteps on the central stairs and didn't envy his daughter, although she doubted the girl she'd met would be so easily cowed.

In fact, Tiree was rooting for young Eloise despite the girl's rudeness. With an autocrat like Sinclair for a father, who could blame her for being difficult?

Not that Tiree had much experience of fathers, full stop. The commune, in which she'd been reared until eleven, had been largely matriarchal. Men had come and gone. A couple had even come and stayed, but they'd had little to do with the upbringing of the children.

Arguably, no one had. With anarchy being the prevailing philosophy, the children had been allowed to do pretty much as they liked, apart from a few hours schooling and that possibly had been more to do with appeasing the local education office. Music was more highly regarded and Tiree had learned the violin at the knee of a woman who had once played for an orchestra.

While doubting she would ever choose to bring her own children up in such an environment, Tiree had mainly happy memories of the place. With communal childcare arrangements and discouragement of insular families, she had not stuck out from the rest. Everyone used first names, so it had mattered less that she couldn't call anyone "mum". If anything, her origins were deemed to make her the special one. She was "a gift", left in sacred trust: the embodiment of the commune's principles.

So there she'd been, living in cloud-cuckoo-land, when the real world had finally intruded. At first it came in the shape of a local policeman, sent to investigate what even he called a preposterous story. A woman in a hospital in Glasgow was claiming to have abandoned a child on the commune doorstep. No record of the child could be found so he assumed it was all a fiction.

Panicked, the commune had agreed. There was no such child. They'd felt unable to do otherwise, having failed to ever register their 'gift', and they'd hoped the problem would just go away. It hadn't.

The next visitor was from social services. The woman had since died of kidney failure but without recanting her story. The commune was faced with a choice: coming clean or facing a more rigorous investigation that might lead to prosecution. No choice really. Tiree accepted that, even if she'd been the one left to suffer the consequences.

Under the auspices of social services, Tiree had gained an identity but lost a home. It wasn't as if there were any eager relatives to take her in: her mother had been the only child of older parents, long since deceased, who had turned their back on her when she became pregnant; her father was an unknown entity. Yet, despite her pleas, the authorities had refused to allow her to remain with the commune.

The only concession given was her name. She had to be registered. She could use the one bestowed on her by the commune or be Amy Ross as her mother had called her. Having lost everything else, she had chosen to cling on to Tiree Nemo, even if it had occasioned scorn in the children's home, her next port of call.

Tiree could still recall her first day there. She'd arrived, clutching a black bin-bag of her possessions and wearing baggy trousers and a knitted jumper like the hippie child she was. She'd been shaking inside, unused to strangers, but had attempted a brave smile at the children who'd gathered round her, seeming to offer friendship.

The laughter had started the second her social worker left. Everything about her, it had appeared, was funny. Her clothes. Her lilting accent. Her long braided hair. The threadbare teddy they'd found in her bag.

Within an hour she was cowering in a corner. Mouse, one of the boys had christened her, and Mouse she had remained. That boy had been Stu. Later he'd confessed that their cruelty had been envy. Here was someone who'd once had a decent life. Here was someone who was probably just passing through.

They'd been right. A month of bullying—not long enough to really toughen her up—and she'd been out of there. Social services had gone through the motions of consulting her.

Would she like to be fostered? In other words, would she like a get-out-of-jail-free card? Yes, please.

Forget that she had no real idea what it entailed. A visit to the Chisolms: woman warm and welcoming, man more circumspect. Total strangers one day, living in their house the next. And she was reckoned to be one of the fortunate ones.

The other children had certainly thought so. They'd seen the photograph album of the Chisolms and their big posh villa in the West End. She'd hit the jackpot. Lucky cow.

The only dissenting voice had been Stu's. Normally he'd treated her with offhand contempt, but this time he'd deigned to comment, 'It's more difficult than you realise.'

'What is?'

'Foster care.'

'Worse than this?' With an alternative in sight, Tiree had grown bold enough to admit her dislike of Sunnydale House.

Sunnydale? What a joke! Nothing sunny about this Victorian pile.

'Sometimes.' One word, gravely delivered from the boy who was rarely serious.

A moment's doubt as she'd looked into eyes which had already seen too much of the world. Did he know something that she didn't?

'You can say no,' he'd added. 'They can't make you go.'

It had broken the spell. Tiree had assumed the advice malevolent.

'You'd like that, wouldn't you?' she'd thrown back. 'Have me stay here, just so I can be as miserable as you. Well... Well, to hell with you, Stu Maclennan!'

It was the first time she'd used bad language and it had felt strangely liberating. It wouldn't be the last.

Not that it had much affect on Stu. He'd probably come out of the womb swearing. But he'd chosen to laugh rather than hit her, the more common resolution to arguments around Sunnydale.

'The Mouse that roared,' he'd scoffed, and the other kids had started doing roaring noises in her face.

Stu had looked on, grinning like a Roman emperor who'd

just released the lions. Tiree had hated him that day, but never forgotten him. How could she when his words had turned out to be prophetic. Living with the Chisolms certainly had been difficult at times and bloody awful by the end.

But Tiree put a brake on her thoughts there. It wasn't a road she allowed herself down these days. It led nowhere but a dead end and she didn't need the grief.

Instead she turned her concentration on to food. The appetite she had lost after the car accident had suddenly returned.

She raided fridge, freezer and cupboards to come up with a pretty good idea of Sinclair's eating habits. A rabid meat eater, he dined on casseroles prepared and packaged by his house-keeper.

Tiree would have probably given them a wide berth even if she hadn't been a vegetarian. Instead she prepared her own concoction of pasta, cheese, peppers and some tired-looking mushrooms in the fridge, adding a liberal amount of herbs to give it some kick. She catered for three, but didn't wait to help herself to a portion, washing it down with some mineral water.

She was just finishing when Sinclair finally did reappear. He looked as if he had the world on his shoulders from which Tiree concluded his tête-à-tête with young Miss Sinclair had not gone well.

He caught her enquiring look but simply muttered, 'Don't ask.'

'Okay, I won't.' She indicated the dish. 'Want some?'

He studied the contents with some suspicion but eventually said, 'Yes, all right.'

Tiree forgave him his lack of enthusiasm. He'd had a hard day. Hadn't they all?

'I'll warm it up.' She carried the dish to the microwave and, putting it on for a couple of minutes, pretended great interest in the motion of the turntable.

Behind her, Sinclair had crossed to the fridge and was check-ing out the contents. He took out a couple of chilled bottles of lager.

'I'm having a beer. Would you like one?' he offered as she carried the heated dish back to the table and sat down again.

'No, thanks.'

'Wine, then?'

Tiree considered this alternative but decided against it. 'I think I'll just stick to water.'

Sinclair caught the slight grimace on her face and enquired, 'Headache?'

She shook her head, not wishing for sympathy, but his eyes remained on her as he took the chair opposite.

Tiree ignored this open scrutiny and served him a portion of the pasta.

He took another sip from his beer bottle before eating, tentatively at first, then with apparent enjoyment.

'Like it?' Tiree preened herself on her culinary skills.

He looked across at her in surprise. 'You made it?'

'Who else?' enquired Tiree.

'I assumed Mrs Enderby,' Sinclair admitted, 'although, it's not her usual fare.'

'So I gathered from your freezer,' Tiree countered. 'You do know a diet of red meat clogs up your arteries—not to mention what it does to the poor cows?'

'A vegetarian! I might have guessed,' Sinclair concluded in return. 'I suppose it's very trendy these days among celebrity types.'

'*Trendy*?' echoed Tiree. 'Well, that word certainly isn't. And, in point of fact, I've always been a vegetarian.'

'Always? Even when you were a child?'

She nodded. 'No choice in the matter. The whole commune was.'

'Ah, yes, I forgot about *the commune*,' he repeated as if doubting its existence, 'on whose doorstep you happened to appear.'

He made it sound highly unlikely, but Tiree couldn't help that. She'd told him the truth—something she didn't always do. If he chose to disbelieve, that was up to him.

'So why isn't this mentioned in the newspapers?' he drawled on. 'The potted biography I read claimed you were brought up by a single mother in a Glasgow tenement... A good rags-toriches story, granted, but surely your version would be even more sensational?'

Tiree agreed, but, of course, he'd missed the point. Unable to see past her professional image, he assumed she would welcome such sensation. He just didn't know her.

Didn't want to know her, either, Tiree suspected. So why explain herself?

'Forget it, okay.' She shrugged her indifference.

'Okay.' He smiled as if he'd won his point.

Men were such boys, Tiree thought.

She changed the subject, saying, 'I'll heat another plate's worth if you want to take it up to your daughter. She can't have eaten.'

His face took on a stubborn set. 'She can come down if she's hungry.'

'I see.' Tiree resisted any impulse to comment.

He still read criticism in her tone. 'It's she who's sulking with me. I tried reasoning with her.'

'I can imagine,' Tiree murmured back.

Blue eyes narrowed on her. 'What's that supposed to mean?'

'Nothing.' Tiree was sure he could work it out for himself.

Sinclair kept his mouth tightly clamped, fighting a temptation to justify himself as a father. And to this girl, of all people? Not exactly Mary Poppins material, was she?

She already looked bored with the whole matter. 'Is it all right if I use the telephone? I want to see if I can contact Les.'

Les? The manager, Sinclair recalled.

'You can use the one in my study.' He pushed back his chair and escorted her down the corridor. He switched on the light, allowing her to go past him.

Tiree walked over to the desk where the telephone sat. She did not, however, pick up the receiver. She was waiting for Sinclair, still lurking in the doorway, to leave.

Instead he said, 'I trust you'll be discreet and not mention my name, bearing in mind your manager may be the mole.'

'Yes, all right! Don't worry!' Tiree sighed expressively. She'd got the message—maybe half a dozen times. 'Anyway, I don't know your name, apart from the Sinclair bit.'

'Ewan,' he replied with some hesitation, 'although friends tend to call me Sinclair or Sinc.'

'Right.' Tiree didn't think she'd be using Sinc any time soon or Ewan, for that matter. 'Your parents are Scottish, I take it.'

'Were,' he corrected. 'My mother died of cancer when I was fourteen, and my father a few years later from heart failure.'

'Tough,' Tiree ventured in comment.

He shrugged. 'It didn't really affect my life as such. My parents were abroad a great deal—diplomatic service. I spent much of my childhood at boarding school.'

Which presumably had the development of a stiff upper lip high on its curriculum.

'And yours?' he added, hoping to catch her off guard.

'My what?' Tiree gave him an enquiring look.

'Parents,' he supplied.

Tiree shrugged. 'My mother's dead. That's definite.'

'How do you know?' he asked. 'Considering you were left on a doorstep, I mean.'

Was that scepticism talking?

Tiree told him all the same. 'She made a deathbed confession, and the facts checked out. Unfortunately it was too late for the grand reunion.'

She left the choice of believing up to him.

Her manner was flippant, her eyes hard, yet Sinclair found himself wondering if this fanciful story could actually be the truth.

'What about your father?'

'Unknown and likely to remain so.'

She didn't sound as if she cared, but Sinclair had enough imagination to figure how deeply it might hurt, being abandoned in such a fashion.

Tiree caught his gaze. Great! So now he was contemplating pitying her?

'Anyway, *Ewan*,' she destroyed the moment with intentional sarcasm, 'now we've empathised, could I use your telephone?'

'Just stick to Sinclair.' Blue eyes instantly lost their sympathetic hue as they narrowed on her, before he turned and left.

He didn't exactly slam the door. He was too restrained and uptight for that. But his departure was certainly abrupt.

It was so easy to yank his chain, Tiree smirked to herself, as she dialled Les's London flat.

Her smile faded as the telephone rang and rang until it switched to the answering machine. She tried her cottage next.

This time there were three rings at most before the receiver was lifted and a familiar voice demanded, 'Is that you, Ti? Where the hell are you?'

'That doesn't matter.' Tiree felt she owed Sinclair some discretion. 'Are there reporters still at the cottage?'

'No, they've all gone,' Les assured her, 'but they'll probably be back. Is it true? You've had a fall down stairs? How are you feeling?'

There was concern in his voice but Tiree wasn't altogether sure of its origin. Les was a businessman, first and last, and she was his commodity.

'I'm fine,' she dismissed, 'I slipped on the stairs and knocked myself out, that's all. There's no real damage, just a bump on my head and a few bruises. But I've decided to take a rest, maybe go away for a while.'

There was a silence on the other end as Les chose his words carefully. 'Listen, I know it's been a stressful time for you, Ti, but I'm not sure I'd advise a career break at this stage. The single could well reach number one this Sunday, and, if you're going to capitalise on that, you'll have to make some appearances.'

'Appearances on what?' Tiree echoed in disbelief.

'TV. Radio. Maybe do an interview with a sympathetic tabloid,' Les rattled off. 'Just say the word and I'll arrange it. Also, the record company wants a meeting to discuss your transition to a solo artist.'

From Les's tone he clearly expected her to be excited at the prospect. Instead she was appalled. Stu and Kit were barely cold in their graves.

'I don't want to be a solo artist.' Her tone should have told him she didn't want to be any kind of artist.

'I understand,' Les claimed although he clearly didn't, 'and that isn't a problem. We need a new line-up for the American tour, anyway. You and Wayne, of course, and I was thinking a couple of session musicians on guitar, maybe, or better still, if we could find someone established—'

Tiree couldn't tolerate listening to more. She put the handset down on its cradle, effectively ending the conversation. Possibly ending her career, too.

The relief was heady.

CHAPTER FIVE

'EVERYTHING all right?' Sinclair found her sitting motionless by the phone.

Tiree, who had been a million miles away, dragged herself back to the here and now. 'Yes, fine.'

'You talked to your manager?' he prompted, trying to gauge her mood.

She nodded. 'Les says the Press have gone.'

'Temporarily, I imagine,' he commented. 'Is this Les coming for you?'

'No.' Tiree would be quite happy if she never saw Les again. 'You're stuck with me... At least for tonight.'

Sinclair raised no objection but asked, 'Will Eloise do as a chaperone? It's rather late to call Mrs Enderby out.'

'Sure.' The chances of him making a pass at her seemed remote; that earlier kiss now seemed surreal.

'I'll show you to the guest room.' He led the way up the stairs.

She followed in his wake, still limping slightly. Strains of rock music became louder as they climbed. Tiree identified the album being played—it was Kinetic Sugar's last. She wondered if Sinclair was aware of it.

There were several doors off the first-floor landing. She guessed which was his daughter's, not just from the music, but the tray with licked-clean plate outside. So he had given way and brought her dinner while she'd been on the telephone.

He caught her glance. 'She had to eat.'

'Of course.' He didn't need to justify himself to Tiree. She would have done the same.

'Wait here a second.' He entered another room and came back with a pair of man's pyjamas. 'I'm afraid it's all I have.'

Tiree took the clothes and murmured an almost gracious, 'Thanks.'

'This way.' There was another flight of stairs to the attic floor. He opened a door but didn't go in. 'There's a key in the lock. Not that you'll need to use it.'

He awarded her one of his haughty I-wouldn't-touch-you-with-a-barge-pole looks. It was as convincing as it was insulting.

'Great.' She waited for him to leave.

But he was clearly working his way round to saying something else. 'I'd like to think I could trust you, too.'

'Don't flatter yourself!' Tiree scoffed in response. 'Even tarts have their limits.'

For a moment Sinclair was at a loss. It hadn't even occurred to him that *she'd* be interested in *him*.

'Glad to hear it,' he smiled briefly, 'but that wasn't quite what I meant. I'm more concerned that you don't decide to disappear in the night. You may feel absolutely fine, but you did have a concussion.'

'Right, I'm with you now…and the answer is no, I'm not currently planning a moonlight flit,' she volunteered, quickly covering her embarrassment.

'Good,' he nodded shortly.

'Still,' Tiree couldn't resist adding, 'if I change my mind, I promise I won't touch the family silver.'

Sinclair sighed heavily. Was this girl never serious about anything?

He studied her face while she looked back at him, unblinking. Her eyes were hard but beautiful, too, an unusual green, fringed by dark, sweeping lashes. All her features had a delicate kind of beauty. Only when she spoke, did the porcelain-doll image give way to the cheap-looking girl who fronted a rock band.

Tiree assumed they were having a staring-out contest until his gaze switched to her mouth. She pouted, insolent rather provocative, but when he raised his eyes back to her face, there was desire in the way he looked at her.

He didn't hide it, and, Tiree, wondering why she'd ever thought this man cold, was thrown for a moment.

Sinclair, however, was quite familiar with his own, quite

healthy, sex drive. It was the target that caught him by surprise. Maybe he *was* going through a mid-life crisis, wanting to bed younger women, regardless.

The thought, as unwelcome as it was, helped restore sanity and he picked up the thread of the conversation, almost growling at her, 'I'll say goodnight, then,' before turning on his heel.

Tiree was left feeling curiously abandoned. She watched his retreating back and considered what had just happened. Very little. An exchange of looks, making her imagine more. But, in essence, nothing.

So why was he angry again?

Tiree shook her head, a shade angry herself, and decided not to dwell on it, as she disappeared into her room for the night.

She switched on an overhead light and surveyed her accommodation. Double bed with carved wooden panels. Antique, possibly. A floral cover that matched the curtains. Bedside cabinets, both with lamps, and an oak wardrobe with drawers underneath. It was comfortable but depersonalised, like a bedroom in some upmarket country-house hotel.

Not that the decor mattered. She wasn't planning a long stay. Six hours sleep and she was out of here.

First, she had to take care of practicalities. She went through to the *en suite* bathroom and took a quick shower—wonderfully hot—before trying the pyjamas.

Striped cotton—did men still wear these?—they swamped her. Not surprising. He was a head taller. She discarded the bottoms and settled for the top as a nightshirt.

It got her thinking about what she was going to wear when she escaped Casa Sinclair tomorrow. She'd washed her underwear and draped it over a radiator. Her jeans weren't too bad— no more crumpled and disreputable than jeans were intended to look—but the borrowed polo shirt was too large to be worn without attracting some notice.

She thought of her wet T-shirt. She'd taken it in from the car but left it downstairs, draped over a radiator in the kitchen. She decided to go down and fetch it. She trusted that Sinclair would be already tucked up in bed and asleep.

The house was certainly dark and silent as the grave as she

crept downstairs, holding onto the banister for guidance, so it came as a bit of a shock when she entered the kitchen to find she was not alone in her night-time wandering.

At least it was Eloise, rather than her father, sitting at the table, spooning ice cream out of a tub.

'Hungry?' she suggested with a friendly smile.

The girl's expression was wary in return. 'I suppose you'll go off and tell my dad.'

'Tell him what?' Tiree echoed. 'I assume you're not going to pull a disappearing act dressed in pyjamas and slippers.'

'No!' Sullen eyes took in Tiree's own night attire. 'Is that my dad's?'

Tiree nodded. 'I'm staying in the guest room,' she stated in case Eloise had other ideas.

She crossed to pick up her T-shirt from the radiator, and the girl directed at her back, 'You're really not his latest, then?'

She turned and gave a slight sigh, 'I'm sure your father has told you otherwise.'

Eloise shrugged. 'I asked who you were but he wouldn't say... You're not another au pair, are you?'

Tiree shook her head. 'Do you normally have one?'

'We used to,' Eloise relayed, 'only the last one—Isabella— she was a mega-embarrassment.'

A pause followed, inviting curiosity, but Tiree remained silent.

Eloise continued, regardless, 'I mean she was okay at first, apart from gibbering on in Spanish a bit—'

'Because she was Spanish maybe?' Tiree interjected with a touch of irony.

'I suppose.' Eloise directed her a pained look that asked if she wanted to hear the story or not.

Tiree wasn't sure she did. It wasn't any of her business. But she found herself sinking into the seat opposite Eloise's.

'Anyway—' the girl ran on '—she only goes off and falls for my dad. We're talking the real thing here. Watches him when she thinks no one is looking. Goes pink every time he says as much as pass the gravy. Starts asking him all kind of stupid things just to talk to him. Too, too obvious! Not that

Dad noticed. Well, not until it became so in-your-face even he couldn't miss it. Silly cow!' the girl dismissed contemptuously.

'I take it this story doesn't have a happy-ever-after ending,' Tiree concluded, slightly sceptical about its veracity.

'Hardly. He sacked her in the end—' Eloise pulled a face '—and I was forced to go to boarding school.'

Enlightenment dawned. The real issue wasn't lovesick Spanish girls or the embarrassment they caused, but the impact on Eloise.

'Which you don't like?' figured Tiree.

'*Like*?' Eloise almost spat the word. 'Have you ever been to a boarding school?'

No, arguably Tiree had been to worse, a council-run care home, but she decided any count-yourself-lucky anecdote would be lost on Eloise.

'It's awful!' The girl emphasised the point by digging at her ice cream as if the spoon was an offensive weapon. 'No, it's worse than awful. It's like prison, only you haven't done anything to deserve being locked up, so you get angry all the time,' she ended resentfully.

Even allowing for twelve-year-old drama-queen tendencies, Eloise Sinclair was clearly one unhappy girl.

'Perhaps you should explain to your dad how you feel?' Tiree suggested.

Eloise snorted. 'Yeah, and he's going to listen?'

Clearly not in her opinion.

Tiree, who had not found Sinclair the most sympathetic ear, resisted the temptation to commiserate.

'I bet it suits him, anyway,' Eloise sniffed. 'With me gone, he can have his girlfriends to stay.'

'That's assuming he has any.' Tiree couldn't picture Sinclair a serial philanderer for all that she'd caught glimpses of a nature more sexual than his pompous manner would suggest.

Eloise awarded her a 'do you think I'm naïve' look. 'Of course he has girlfriends. Women are always throwing themselves at him,' the girl claimed with perverse pride. 'Even my friends think he's good-looking. For an old guy, that is.'

Tiree supposed the girl had a point. Ignore his actual personality, and, on a purely physical level, Sinclair could be the subject of many females' fantasy.

'In fact, I caught one once,' Eloise confided, 'coming out of his room. It was four in the morning, I'd got up to go to the toilet and there she was, this Stephanie woman from his hospital. Boy, did she look guilty!'

Tiree considered offering an innocent explanation but couldn't think of one, so she asked instead, 'Did you mind?'

Eloise considered the question before shrugging, 'Not really. I know some girls do. That's why they're packed off to school, so they can't make trouble about their mum or dad's new partner. But I don't remember my mum... Anyway, I told him it was cool.'

'You did?' That must have been an interesting conversation.

'Not that I let on or anything,' Eloise explained. 'It was the woman who told him. He felt quite bad about it but there was no need. I understand about these things.'

Tiree resisted a smile and said, 'You're obviously mature for your age.'

Eloise looked pleased that someone appreciated the fact. Pleased enough to press, 'Are you definitely not a girlfriend?'

Tiree shook her head. 'Totally definitely. The truth is much more boring. Last night I fell downstairs and knocked myself out. I also sprained my ankle which made it impossible to drive so my doctor, realising we lived quite close to each other, asked your father to run me home.'

'But you're here?' Eloise immediately saw the inconsistency.

Tiree thought quickly. 'Yes, well, that's because your father stopped off to pick up something, then you turned up, time went on, and it became simpler for me to stay here rather than talk you out of your room.'

'Sorry.' Eloise made a face of apology.

'It's all right,' Tiree shrugged. 'I had nothing planned for the evening.'

At this Eloise came to the conclusion, 'So you're not married or anything?'

'No, why?'

'I was thinking…well, if you were to fancy my dad, it would be cool. I mean you seem okay.'

Tiree shook her head. 'Just passing through, I'm afraid.'

'Pity!' Eloise sighed. 'I was hoping you might then persuade Dad that I won't interfere with his private life if he lets me stay at home.'

Tiree questioned if the girl was being quite fair. 'Are you sure that's why he sent you away to school?'

'Well, maybe not the only reason,' Eloise conceded. 'The trouble was, when soppy Isabella went back to Barcelona, there was no one to collect me from school or babysit if he was called out. Mrs Enderby, that's our housekeeper, filled in for a while but she's kind of ancient, and it was getting too much for her so he decided boarding school was the answer.'

Eloise clearly thought it the wrong answer but Tiree appreciated it was a difficult situation for Sinclair. 'Is he taking you back tomorrow?'

The girl nodded gloomily. 'Unless I get lucky and the school expels me.'

'Was that the master plan,' Tiree surmised, 'in running away?'

'No!' Eloise seemed genuinely indignant at the suggestion.

Tiree raised an appeasing hand. 'Okay, I believe you.'

'Honestly,' Eloise stressed, 'it was just…well, I couldn't stand it any more. This week, especially.'

'Of course.' Tiree assumed that was a reference to the coroner's enquiry.

Eloise confirmed as much in asking, 'Do you know about my brother, Kit?'

Even as she nodded, Tiree hoped Eloise wouldn't ask her how and what she knew. The girl hadn't an inkling who she was and it seemed preferable to leave things that way.

'Well, I'd told a few of the girls that my brother played for Kinetic Sugar,' Eloise added. 'Showing off, I suppose. Only after the accident and all the stuff in the papers, I wished I hadn't, because the whole school knows now and everybody keeps asking me idiotic questions.'

'Maybe they're trying to be sympathetic?' hazarded Tiree.

'Some, yes,' Eloise agreed, 'but others just want to know whether I've met Ti Nemo and can I get her autograph... I mean it's really sick, as if they don't understand my brother's dead and won't ever come back again.'

The girl's voice finally broke and her blue eyes filled with tears. Tiree came round the table to sit at her side.

'It's all right. Cry if you want—' she laid a gentle arm on hers '—no one to hear but me.'

The girl stiffened momentarily, then her shoulders began to heave and grief overcame her.

Tiree did not question that this blasé almost-teenager could so quickly turn into a wretched child. She remembered being the same way herself. Well, until life had toughened her up and she'd lost the ability to cry.

She could still offer comfort and gently stroked the girl's hair, making soothing noises as Eloise burrowed her head in her shoulder, and accepted the mothering offered.

To Sinclair, however, it seemed strange. Brought downstairs for a nightcap, he stood rooted in the doorway and watched Ti Nemo as she rocked his distraught daughter with a compassion that he would not have imagined her possessing.

Yet maybe he was the one lacking for Eloise had failed to turn to him earlier.

Even now he hesitated. It was a long time since Eloise had climbed on his knee for a reassuring cuddle or come to him in tears, certain he could solve all her problems. Would she welcome his intervention at this stage?

At length Tiree sensed the presence of a third party and, looking up, caught Sinclair's eye. She made a slight gesture, signalling that she would leave and allow him to take over, but he shook his head and, observing the scene a moment longer, turned on his heel and was gone.

Tiree frowned after him, surprised he would entrust her with a weeping Eloise. Or was he so emotionally repressed he'd rather risk her influence than cope with a few tears?

Poor Eloise. Tiree worried for her future. Starved of love, young girls tended to go looking and find it in the wrong places.

But what could she do? Nothing. She was just passing through.

Still she gave Eloise her time, waiting until her sobs tailed off into hiccups, before saying, 'You need to sleep.'

A mumbled, 'Yes,' and the girl let Tiree support her upstairs.

They passed Sinclair's room, door ajar and the light on, and continued along to the girl's. Tiree noted the rosettes and pony pictures on one wall, and the pop posters on the other. A room in transition, much like Eloise.

She drew back the duvet, saying, 'Hop in,' and tucked it round her when she was in bed. 'You're a bit too old for a story, I suppose.'

Eloise acknowledged the fact with a slight smile, suggesting, 'Music would be nice.'

'Okay but I choose.' Tiree sorted through the pile of CDs on a bookcase, avoiding Kinetic Sugar and some pretty heavy rap music, in favour of a girl group with sweet voices and unthreatening lyrics.

She put it on low volume and Eloise said, 'Stay and listen if you like.'

Tiree met appealing blue eyes and understood. Eloise wanted company a little while longer. So she sat on a bedside chair and pretended an interest in the music until she saw Eloise's eyelids gradually droop, then close.

Tiree could have drifted off herself but the chair wasn't that comfortable, so she waited a few minutes to be sure Eloise was asleep before creeping out of the bedroom.

The floorboards creaked and alerted the man listening out for her.

He appeared abruptly and startled her a little. 'Sorry, I didn't mean to frighten you.'

But Tiree was already recovering, claiming, 'You didn't,' before relaying, 'She's asleep.'

He nodded in appreciation. 'Why exactly was she crying?'

'Kit, mainly,' Tiree volunteered, 'and the fact that the girls at school are proving less than sensitive about his death.'

Sinclair frowned. He'd tried to discuss such matters with

Eloise and she'd just shrugged. It seemed she felt more able to open up to a total stranger.

Why? Was he so unapproachable? Or was there something special about this woman, with her sloping green eyes that seemed almost catlike in this light?

He felt drawn to her, too, but it was hardly the same thing. With him the attraction was physical. Even now, worried as he was about Eloise, another part of him was acutely aware of Ti Nemo and the fact she was probably naked under the pyjama top she wore.

He sought refuge in formality, 'Thank you for your consideration towards Eloise,' and, receiving one of her are-you-for-real stares in return, tried not to watch as she climbed the further staircase and afforded him a view of slender, shapely legs that only made him wonder harder about the rest of her.

What had Eloise said? 'She's cute, your latest, but maybe a little young?'

He'd refused to react, of course, at this attempt to annoy. Eloise must have known Ti Nemo was certainly not *his* latest, young or no. He couldn't dispute the cute, although, like his pyjama top, it seemed barely adequate to cover the girl's charms.

He shook his head, putting a brake on such thoughts, and switched back to the more important issue of Eloise.

Very quietly he entered his daughter's bedroom. She was sound asleep. Feeling a profound protective love for her, he placed a kiss on her forehead and saw her tear-stained cheeks as a reproach. He'd imagined that, after the initial shock, she was coping well with Kit's death. But what did he really know? The lines of communication between them had been down long before that.

It had been so much easier when she was younger. When Nicole had walked out on him for good, Eloise had just been a baby, a lucky accident from their reconciliation. He'd fought for custody and won. His circumstances had offered the more stable home and the blood tie had weighed in his favour where its absence had counted against him in Kit's case. Housekeepers and au pairs had taken care of the practicalities, and for a long time they'd been closer than most fathers and daughters, his occasional woman friends having to take second place.

He supposed the change had been inevitable, although he hadn't been ready for it. One moment he was living with a fairly reasonable, eminently likeable eleven-year-old, the next a sub-teen dedicated to sulking and arguing and desperate to dress like a vamp.

He could have coped but it seemed the average au pair couldn't. They'd either let her run riot or ran themselves. Isabella from Spain was the final straw. A pleasant if nervous girl, she had become so unhinged she had ended up professing undying love for him. Not wishing to repeat that experience, he'd relied on Mrs Enderby, but, of course, Eloise had proved too much for her as well.

Boarding school had seemed the obvious answer. Familiar territory to him—he'd attended one from the age of eight— he'd believed that it would offer the consistency her life lacked. Unfortunately Eloise had seen it as some kind of punishment and had run away three times so far, showing no sign of settling as the headmistress promised. The issue had rapidly become a battlefield, with neither prepared to retreat.

Even now, though he wished for his daughter's happiness, Sinclair doubted the efficacy of simply letting her leave. It was no doubt what Ti Nemo would advocate: a don't-like-it, don't-do-it policy. But Sinclair was governed by different principles, an amalgam of duty, responsibility and self-denial.

On the floor above, Tiree was coping with her own demons. She'd promised herself not to go down this road again but Eloise's unhappiness had brought it all flooding back again. Tiree knew too well how it felt to be twelve and at the mercy of the adult world.

It was the age she'd gone to live with the Chisolms. They'd seemed a nice, respectable, middle-class couple and she'd been sold as pretty, smart and anxious to please. Social services had high hopes for the placement.

So had Tiree. What girl wouldn't be impressed by a beautifully decorated bedroom in a posh West End villa and a place in one of the best private schools in Glasgow?

Tiree had kept telling herself how lucky she was and, like a mantra, it worked for a while. So what if Margaret preferred to have things done in a certain way, to control what Tiree wore and ate and thought? Perhaps that was normal in normal families. And if Tom Chisolm seemed indifferent in contrast, Tiree was surely not going to complain.

In fact, how could she? The only forum was a three-monthly review and with Margaret sitting in, Tiree couldn't bring herself to voice any dissatisfaction.

Things went sour all the same. She couldn't pinpoint a time. It was more gradual. She'd tried hard to love Margaret. She'd called her 'mummy' as requested, even though it seemed babyish, and aped her way of talking and dressing and thinking, until her head ached with the effort. In her own way, Margaret tried too, but the bond was missing so they settled for a facsimile.

Then one day Tiree overheard a conversation that made even that impossible. It had never been intended for her ears. She'd come home early from her Saturday violin lesson and followed the sound of their voices to the terrace outside. Realising they were mid-quarrel, Tiree had stopped short at the French windows. She was then held there by a grim fascination.

Tom to Margaret: *'It wasn't my idea to foster.'*

Margaret to Tom: *'You agreed.'*

Tom to Margaret: *'I agreed to adopt a baby. Tiree is far from that. Not that you seem to have noticed.'*

Margaret to Tom: *'What do you mean?'*

Tom to Margaret: *'The way you treat her. Like she's three years old.'*

Margaret to Tom: *'I do not, and even if I did she doesn't mind. The social worker said these children like to regress.'*

Tom to Margaret: *'That one doesn't. You can see it in her eyes, even when she's saying Yes, please and No, thank you. It's all pretence. And who can blame her?'*

Margaret to Tom: *'You've never taken to her, have you?'*

Tom to Margaret: *'And you have?'*

Margaret to Tom: *'What are you saying?'*

A silence in which Tiree could have chosen to walk away but no, she had to stay around to the bitter end.

Tom to Margaret: *'You might fool the world, Maggie, but you don't fool me. You'd swap her tomorrow for a baby, so don't deny it.'*

Margaret to Tom: *'That isn't true, and even if it was, there are no babies. It's children like Tiree or nothing.'*

Tom to Margaret: *'Then maybe it should have been nothing.'*

Another silence. Tiree waited and waited for Margaret to say something, anything, to make her feel wanted, but all she could hear was the sound of her foster-mother crying.

She was still at the window when Tom suddenly appeared. She had no time to hide, no time to pretend she hadn't been eavesdropping.

They looked at each other through the glass, and for once it was real between them. No false smiles. No gaze shifting. Just the truth exchanged between stares.

Remarkably they'd played Happy Families for another two years. Margaret wasn't one to admit failure and Tiree had no great desire to go rushing back to Sunnydale.

But Tiree had stopped trying after that. No point. How could she ever be Margaret's perfect daughter? She wasn't the baby Margaret craved. She wasn't even the sweet, docile child Margaret preferred. So she slipped back to being the real Tiree, neither bad nor good, clever but not studious, even-tempered but with a definite mind of her own.

Margaret didn't like it, of course. Little by little, treats disappeared, communication faltered and resentment grew.

Conversely, Tiree's relationship with Tom improved. He began to take her out, put an affectionate arm round her, sympathise when Margaret was in one of her screaming moods.

Tiree took this attention at face value. Perhaps it was innocent initially, no hidden agenda, but over time the arm became hugs held a little long, the kiss on the cheek coming closer to her lips. He would tell her how pretty she was and give her extra pocket money with an instruction to keep it from Margaret. She'd smile awkwardly at the compliments and take the money, because it was easier than refusing; she'd even thought there was something wrong with her that she squirmed at Tom's touch.

Was it a shock when Tom eventually crossed the line? Both yes and no. It was as if she'd been going round with blurred vision and had suddenly been granted twenty-twenty.

It had happened after a family wedding. Tom had been drinking steadily despite black looks from Margaret. Tiree had sensed a quarrel brewing and had hung out with an older boy cousin. He was seventeen, she was almost fifteen, and, when he'd started to chat her up, she'd been flattered. They'd danced a couple of slow numbers, shuffling on the dance floor with arms draped over each other. Nothing more, but she'd caught a glimpse of Margaret's face, tight with repressed anger.

Margaret never berated her in front of people. Too middle class for that. She waited until they were home again and up in Tiree's bedroom before tearing into her. Did she want people to think she was a slut? Maybe she liked being pawed by boys, but surely she, of all people, understood the consequences. Underage sex and a concealed pregnancy was what led to babies been dumped on doorsteps.

Tiree listened with flaming cheeks and hands that clenched and unclenched in an almost overpowering desire to slap her foster-mother. Of course, she'd guessed the reason she'd been dumped, but she didn't need it rubbed in her face. Nor did she feel a clinch on the dance floor was a precursor to sex. But Margaret didn't give her a chance to answer, ranting and raving until she ran out of steam and stalked away.

It wasn't the first time Margaret had suggested Tiree must be congenitally amoral but Tiree had yet to acquire immunity to these tirades. Feeling the tears well, she sank down on the bed.

Tom appeared moments later. He put his arm round her and listened sympathetically as she poured out her anguish, making soothing noises in response.

She wasn't a slut at all, he told her. She'd just been dancing. And, anyway, it was to be expected that the boys would go after her, she was such a looker. She was mature, too, practically a woman. It was Margaret who was jealous—even of their closeness. Hard to believe sometimes they weren't father and daughter.

But, he continued, it was a good thing, too. Otherwise they could never be anything more. And they both wanted that, didn't they? He could feel her trembling. It was the same for him so how could it be wrong. No need to worry now. It'd be their secret. Margaret had gone out.

Tom's voice had lowered to a whisper in her ear, then his mouth was suddenly on hers, kissing her as he never had before, mistaking her gasp of horror for encouragement as he stuck his tongue inside.

Revolting. All of it. The sour whisky on his breath. The hand squeezing hard on her breast. The utter shame—had she somehow made this happen?

She went rigid, as he pushed her back on the bed and reached under her skirt. With his mouth clamped on hers, she could only scream inside, over and over in the vain hope that he would stop or someone would help her.

The screams, when they came, weren't from her. The hands that dragged him off weren't hers. The rage-filled face that confronted them belonged to Margaret.

At first there was just the relief and the need to breathe again. Then she tried and failed to make sense of Margaret's hysterical shouting.

The word whore was used repetitively. Strange term to use for a man. Bastard, yes. Tiree echoed that, and pervert. But not whore.

Tom was off the bed by that point, unsteady on his feet, but quick-thinking enough to come up with excuses. Tiree had called to him, asked him to sit with her, begun to cry. He'd put an arm round her. She must have misunderstood, started kissing him, pulled him down on the bed.

Tiree had stared in disbelief at Tom, then Margaret. She was sitting there, a fourteen-year-old girl, with pants torn, her skirt still rucked up to her hips and her arms hugged protectively round her. Tears were falling down her face and she was dumb with shock. The truth was there for Margaret to see.

But Margaret had chosen not to see. She had concentrated her abuse on Tiree, because it had hurt less to have a promiscuous foster-daughter than a faithless, child-molester husband.

Tiree had wanted to fight her corner but it was two against one and she had no weapons. So she'd taken flight, down the stairs and out into the night.

It had been dark and cold but no more frightening than her encounter with Tom Chisolm. Later she'd wondered why she hadn't gone to a friend's house, one of the girls from school. At the time she'd just felt too dirty. So she'd wandered into the city and, by some miracle, had survived the night huddled in a doorway.

In the morning, she'd tramped the four miles to Sunnydale, the children's home. Where else was there for her?

She hadn't needed to go into any long explanations. The Chisolms had already beaten her to it. In their version, she'd become increasingly difficult to handle, so much so that when they'd cautioned her against premature sexual activity, she had responded by attempting to compromise Tom. All very plausible coming from an intelligent middle-class couple who had reported her missing because they were concerned for her safety.

Tiree hadn't thought she stood a chance against their lies, especially when her social worker was clearly inclined to believe them. So she'd played into the Chisolms' hands with her sullen defiance, and adopted the role of teenager turned bad.

But she'd stayed angry, a fact noticed by one familiar inmate. Stu. Still there, taller, leaner and meaner, counting the days to release.

'Told you so,' were the first words he said to her, although it was almost three years since their last conversation, 'What happened? Did the father have a go?'

Tiree had been too surprised to deny it. In fact, she'd demanded, 'To whom have you been talking?'

'*To whom*?' he echoed derisively. 'Get you, Miss Milngavie Princess... I don't have to talk to nobody. You think you're the only kid some creep has climbed in with in the night?'

'No.' A pause had followed while Tiree had appreciated the

fact they might be on personal ground here. Not hers, but Stu's. 'So what do you suggest I do?'

A brow was raised at her naïvety. 'You live with it, what else?'

And here she was, eight years on, still living with it. Long after she'd forgotten what Tom Chisolm looked like, she could hear his voice in her head, hoarsely whispering words to convince himself she wanted this, before he tried to rape her. Long after the bruises had faded, she remembered how it had felt to be pinned down on a bed, too frightened to cry out or move.

She knew it could have been worse. She'd met others whom no one had arrived in time to save. But that made no difference. Two minutes' terror at the hands of Tom Chisolm had spoiled each and every relationship she'd had, apart from her one with Stu.

How she missed him. United by a bond only they understood, he'd become her family and she his. Through it all—homelessness, loneliness, fame and despair—they had always been there for each other.

Now here she was, once again adrift, lying in a strange house, listening to night noises until sleep eventually claimed her.

CHAPTER SIX

WITH the curtains purposely left open, sunrise acted as an early morning wake-up call. Tiree opened an eye, squinted at the bright light, then shut it again. She still felt tired and contemplated just rolling into a ball and going back to sleep, but that would make a clean getaway more difficult.

No, best out of here. Throw on her clothes. Underwear dry and wearable. Jeans next. His polo shirt again. Her T-shirt abandoned on a chair after her encounter with Eloise.

Poor kid, but what could she do? Sinclair wasn't going to listen to any advice from her. Easier to leave before the others awoke. Dressed, she stood and tested out her ankle. Any pain was now mild. She went to the window to check on the weather. It was dry and fine.

Tiree was just turning away when her eye caught movement. A car was slowly driving up the lane to the house. She couldn't see the driver but she glanced at her watch. Six-thirty a.m. Too early for his housekeeper surely, but who else would call at such an hour?

She watched until it came to a halt outside the gate. She waited for the driver to climb out and use the intercom at the gate. But no, he or she appeared happy to park.

Tiree's mind began racing. Who else could it be but another of the Press, managing to track her down here? And if there was one, there would soon be more for they hunted in packs.

Her first instinct was to flee down the stairs and out through the back door. The house was silent. She made it, unhindered. She'd slid the bolt and turned the key before she considered what she was doing—leaving Sinclair to clear up her mess.

Still, she hadn't asked him to involve himself, had she? She hadn't forced him to bring her back here. It had been virtual kidnap. So why not let him deal with the consequences?

Tiree had almost won this battle with her conscience when

she thought of Eloise. The girl was already emotionally vulnerable. Did she deserve to wake up to a Press call?

Hand on the bolt, Tiree slotted it back in place. She could spare five minutes, surely? Pre-warned was pre-armed, and all that.

This time she made no attempt to be quiet as she hurried back up the stairs. She knocked on his bedroom door a couple of times but without result. She did not want to call out in case she disturbed Eloise so she entered, regardless.

He was fast asleep on the double bed, lying face up, the duvet pushed down around his waist. It seemed that Sinclair either had only one pair of pyjamas—the ones donated to Tiree—or he didn't normally wear them.

His upper body was lean and muscular, the matt of dark hair on his chest tapering downwards.

Definitely all man.

The phrase slipped into Tiree's head but she was quick to make it slip back out again. If she was cracked enough to start fancying Sinclair, perhaps she *should* be seeing a psychiatrist.

From the side of the bed, she hissed, 'Sinclair.' It had no effect so she hissed more loudly, 'Sinclair, wake up!'

A slight sound came from him, a groan that suggested more pleasure than angst. It occurred to Tiree she might be intruding on a particularly interesting dream.

Making little impression it seemed, as he turned his head into the pillow and went straight back to sleep.

Tiree considered shouting him awake but that might also rouse Eloise.

She rounded the bed, so she could see his face. His mouth was moving slightly but it was in a sleep conversation. Reluctantly she kneeled on the mattress and placed a hand on his shoulder to shake him, gently at first, then more insistently.

At last a result, as he rolled onto his back. Unfortunately he took her with him and, thrown off-balance, she found herself sprawled against the chest she'd earlier been admiring.

Her first instinct was to shrink from him. It was countered by Sinclair's, to close an affectionate arm round the warm body next to his.

'Sinclair!' Not so much a hiss this time as a squeal, of indignation rather than alarm.

But Sinclair was working on his own scenario as he slid a hand down to curve her closer while his lips nuzzled her neck as if on automatic pilot.

'Sin—' The rest was lost as he shifted again.

She was under him now, legs entwined despite the barrier of the duvet, and feeling a spectrum of emotions as his lips sought hers in a kiss that went from sleepy and languorous to hard and forceful the moment desire kicked in.

Tiree understood he wasn't really kissing her but whatever woman featured in his dreams. She knew if she started to struggle, he would let her go. Yet she found herself submitting to the passionate onslaught of his mouth and the hands seeking skin.

Her mind formed the protest *What am I doing?*

She told herself, nothing. It was true. She was just lying there, paralysed, as a hand found its way under the polo shirt and stroked upwards from her ribcage to her breast, cupping its weight, gently squeezing, then using a thumb to make sweet circles of the tip until it was swollen hard.

Tiree's limbs were rigid as always but inside she was fluid, blood coursing like a river, desire rising like sap. So new to her to feel this way, wanting this touching, this loving, imagining ahead: him dragging off her top to put hungry lips to her breast, sucking hard while a hand slid to the ache between her thighs. All the more humiliating when he pulled back from her instead.

For Sinclair, reality had merged with dream some time ago. He knew who he was kissing, whose soft, warm body he was exploring. He stopped while he could, unable to ignore the fact she was more passive than responsive.

He looked into a face that now struck him as flawless. Green eyes stared back at him. Not in the usual bold way. More confused.

Maybe she was wondering if he had taken leave of his senses. Maybe he had.

Tiree expected him to say something. "Sorry", perhaps, or "I thought you were someone else". Even a blunt, "let's have sex''. But he remained silent, his eyes holding hers, a hand still heavy on her ribcage.

What are *we* doing? was the question now. Virtual strangers seeking comfort from one another. Comfort? A euphemism, surely?

She finally pushed him away and he let her. She climbed off the bed and backed towards the door, although she had little fear he was going to pounce. It was still a surprise that a man so stern and remote could also be so sensual, but he was no rapist.

He was now sitting up against the wooden bedstead. His eyes swept from her head to her foot but only to challenge, 'You're dressed. Why?'

'It's morning,' she said a little lamely, then remembered why she had entered his room in the first place. 'We may have a problem.'

'Don't tell me—' he raised an eyebrow '—you can't open the front door?'

He'd guessed she was mid-flight. Tiree didn't bother denying it.

Instead she stated, 'Actually I was going to use the back door but I thought I'd better warn you first—there's a reporter parked out front.'

'Damn!' He was suitably rattled but Tiree didn't expect him to react quite as he did.

The covers were pushed back as he rose to get dressed.

Tiree stared for a moment, shocked—yes, he did sleep in the nude—before quickly turning her back and stammering, 'I-I-I'll…um…wait for you in the corridor.'

Sinclair smiled a little. Coyness? It was hardly what one expected, but then Ti Nemo was proving altogether unpredictable, not least in the effect she had on him.

It couldn't just be that she was young and pretty. If he was simply after that, he could take up some of the overtures made to him at the hospital. Arguably not very wise for a man in his position, but neither was trying to seduce volatile female rock singers with a newspaper reporter camped outside.

He shook his head at this aberration and, knotting a tie above a clean white shirt and his suit trousers, took on his normal cloak of responsibility, before going to join her. She was no longer upstairs but down in the hall, looking ready to bolt at the first opportunity.

'Did you tell that manager of yours where you were?' he asked as he reached the bottom step.

Tiree almost welcomed this resumption in hostilities, snapping back, 'No, I did not. If you're looking for a leak, try the hospital.'

Sinclair didn't dispute the possibility.

'Stay here,' he directed, 'while I go out and talk to him.'

Tiree pulled a face at his imperious tone but didn't try to follow as, unlocking the door, he went out into the courtyard. She went through to his study and watched from behind a curtain. He stopped at the gates and eventually a man appeared on the other side. A brief conversation ensued.

Sinclair's next actions confused Tiree totally as he keyed in a code to open the gates and allow the stranger access. They walked towards the house and Tiree studied the other man. About Sinclair's age, he was shorter but quite good-looking, dressed in a smart navy suit and red silk tie. He was laughing about something while Sinclair remained grim-faced.

Tiree heard them enter the hall and listened at the study door.

'You really forgot it?' was enquired on an amused note.

'It's not that funny,' Sinclair countered.

'Oh, but it is!'

'I don't see why... I seem to remember you've missed a few important meetings in your time.'

'Me, yes. More than a few, in fact,' the newcomer confessed. 'But we're talking about you, Mr One-hundred-per-cent Reliable. Just as well I came early.'

'All right, give it a rest, Rhys,' an exasperated Sinclair muttered back.

It was at that point Tiree emerged, realising this Rhys was no reporter.

Sinc's friend acknowledged her with a surprised, then appreciative, look.

'Ah, things are becoming clearer,' he commented in wry tones, 'and a very lovely distraction, too, if I may say so.'

Tiree, unsure if he was talking to her or about her, ignored this obvious flattery and glanced in enquiry at Sinclair.

'It seems I should be attending a conference today.' He was clearly annoyed by his lapse of memory and Tiree realised she probably *had* been the distraction, although not in the way the other man meant it.

'This is Dr Williams, a colleague of mine,' he added shortly.

'A *colleague*? I'm only one of his oldest friends. And it's Rhys, by the way.' A hand was extended to Tiree.

She shook it and a pause followed while they waited, in vain, for Sinclair to complete the introduction.

'I'm Tiree,' she volunteered and could almost hear Sinclair gritting his teeth as she said, 'Tiree Macleod, the new au pair.'

It was a spur of the moment invention, but not bad for all that. Sinclair went from glowering to a much milder frown so she reckoned he approved. In his book, anything was better than her saying who she really was.

'Tiree?' echoed Rhys with interest. 'As in Eigg, Muck and...'

Tiree nodded. 'Do you know Scotland?'

'Spent many a childhood holiday in Argyllshire,' he relayed. 'We'll have to compare notes some time.'

Tiree smiled out of politeness and noticed Sinclair giving her the evil eye once more.

'Perhaps you could make coffee, Tiree?' he suggested heavily.

'Yes, of course, sir.' She bobbed in mock curtsey and turned on her heel, proceeding down the passageway to the kitchen.

She overheard Rhys say, 'Where did you find her? A definite improvement on mad Isabella from Spain.'

'She's temporary,' was Sinclair's clipped response, 'so I wouldn't waste your time chatting her up.'

'I'll bear that in mind—' a chuckle from Rhys deflected his friend's bad temper '—while you shave and I have that coffee.'

An eavesdropping Tiree scuttled into the kitchen and put the kettle on before Rhys appeared. He offered her a smile full of charm and said, 'How long have you been here?'

'Just since last night,' she answered, her manner more reserved.

'And how long are you staying?'

'It hasn't been decided, yet.'

'Student?' he guessed.

'Yes.' A lie seemed easiest.

Only it prompted a further, 'Of what?'

'The violin.' She had been once, in what now seemed the dim and distant past.

'Really.' Rhys raised a brow. 'Quite a trend, these days. Lucrative, too, I believe. Sexy girls and violins.'

Tiree, who didn't think she was looking particularly sexy that morning, temporarily stopped spooning coffee into a cafetière and awarded him an oblique glance. It held mild disdain.

Rhys received the message but managed to shrug it off with a good-natured, 'Well, it certainly helps me to concentrate on my Vivaldi.'

His grin was just self-deprecating enough for Tiree to allow herself a smile in return.

It faltered, however, as she noticed Sinclair in the doorway, glowering and still unshaven.

'What does?' he demanded, having caught the tail-end of the conversation.

'Scantily clad girls playing violin in the sea,' Rhys responded quite happily.

Tiree understood the allusion, having seen the same video as Rhys, but it was lost on Sinclair. Or maybe he was wondering how they had arrived at such a topic when he'd left them alone for less than a minute.

'Well, sorry to break up this intellectual discussion,' he said in a voice laden with sarcasm, 'but, on further reflection, I've decided that you'll have to go to the conference without me.'

'How can I possibly do that?' Rhys was clearly taken aback. 'You're one of the speakers, remember?'

'A *minor* one,' Sinclair claimed modestly. 'I doubt anyone will remark on my absence or even notice if someone else were to deliver my speech.'

He looked meaningfully at Rhys but Rhys was already shaking his head. 'Forget it, pal. My knowledge of childhood TB is minimal and, much as I'd like the kudos, I'm not going to risk exposing my ignorance... What's the problem, anyway?'

Sinclair's eyes strayed in Tiree's direction. He clearly viewed her as part of it.

'I'll be fine.' She forced a smile.

He didn't return it. 'There's Eloise, too.'

'Eloise?' Rhys picked up. 'Don't tell me the schools have broken up for the summer already?'

'Something like that.' Sinclair was in no hurry to advertise his family trouble—even to his friend.

'Surely that's why you've hired Tiree?' Rhys reasoned.

So much for the au pair story. Tiree looked to Sinclair for her cue.

He, in turn, looked aghast at the idea of trusting her with his daughter. What did he imagine she would do in the space of a few hours—corrupt her irredeemably?

She gave an exasperated sigh and, hearing the kettle boil, busied herself with preparing a cafetière of hot coffee.

While she did so, Sinclair came up with the objection, 'Eloise doesn't know Miss Macleod well enough. She only arrived last night.'

'They'll cope, I'm sure, Sinc,' ventured Rhys, adding for Tiree's benefit, 'Eloise is a really nice girl.'

'Yes, she seems it,' agreed Tiree, placing the coffee and cups on the table.

'There you are then.' Matter resolved, Rhys took a seat.

Tiree, dying for a coffee, too, was about to join him when Sinclair appeared at her side to grip her elbow.

'Help yourself, Rhys,' he said in a verisimilitude of politeness, 'while I discuss things with Miss Macleod.'

Tiree was given little chance to object, marched as she was from the kitchen down the hall to the study where they would be out of earshot.

Even then, he got in first, barely shutting the door behind them before exploding, 'What do you think you're doing, pretending to be my au pair, giving him the impression you'll look after Eloise? How do you expect me to get out of the conference now?'

So much for Mr Cool! Tiree felt a distinct sense of superiority.

She might be the one deemed unstable but he was thc one coming apart at the seams.

She resisted saying so, shrugging instead, 'The point is I *will* look after Eloise if you want to go to your conference.'

A genuine offer, it was met with instant suspicion. 'Why would you do that?'

'Why wouldn't I?' she threw back. 'It's no big deal. As your friend says, she's a nice kid.'

'She is, yes,' he echoed before compelled by honesty to add, 'but she can be difficult.'

'I imagine she thinks the same of you,' Tiree dared to suggest.

A ghost of a smile appeared. 'Perhaps.'

'Anyway, it's your choice.' Tiree wasn't going to beg for the privilege. 'I have no plans otherwise and, before you ask: no I won't tell her who I am and yes, I can be relied on to take care of her properly.'

If he was weakening, there was no sign of it. A flicker of annoyance at her reading his thoughts, then his eyes remained centred on hers, trying to read her mind in return. He just couldn't credit that she had no ulterior motives.

It was at this impasse Eloise appeared, bleary-eyed and yawning in the doorway. 'Dad, why's Rhys here?'

'He was going to drive me to a conference in Birmingham,' he explained.

'Oh, right.' Eloise ignored the past tense as her face suddenly brightened. 'Does this mean you can't drive me back to school?'

Tiree felt no surprise at Eloise's reaction. It was bound to be her take on the situation.

Sinclair, who imagined he'd been doing the right thing—sacrificing career and conference for the sake of his daughter—was suitably put out.

'I can't leave you on your own,' he replied heavily.

'No problem,' Eloise dismissed, directing at Tiree, 'You're not going to this boring, old conference, are you?'

'Miss Macleod—' Sinclair began sternly, only to be interrupted.

'Is that your name?' Eloise enquired. 'Do I have to call you that? It makes you sound ancient. Like Mrs Enderby…or Daddy,' she added with a cheeky grin at her father.

Tiree started counting to ten, expecting another explosion from Sinclair, but no, he looked more bemused. Tiree wondered if, excluding the school issue, his daughter usually managed to charm him round.

'Miss Macleod—' he tried again.

This time it was Tiree who chipped in, 'You're right—it makes me sound like some ancient spinster schoolteacher. You can call me Tiree.'

'Tiree?' Eloise echoed, as if it had struck a chord, but to both the adults' relief, she simply added, 'That's different. I like it, though.'

'Thanks,' Tiree smiled.

'We could go out,' Eloise suggested, her mind racing ahead. So was Sinclair's. '*Out*? Out where?'

'Shopping, I imagine.' Tiree knew what twelve-year-old girls liked even if he didn't. 'Unfortunately I've left my purse at home.'

'I have some birthday money left,' Eloise volunteered. 'We could share it… Or Dad could give us some.'

Tiree hesitated, remembering yesterday's Press call at the hospital gates. The photos taken had been of the real her and some might already have been published. It put her at risk of being recognised but, with Eloise's hopeful eyes trained on her, she still nodded in assent.

Sinclair, however, was still struggling with the concept of granting care of his daughter to Ti Nemo.

He gazed at Tiree. Free of make-up, she was a natural beauty with fine-boned features and eyes so green they drew his notice every time he looked at her. A dimpled smile made her seem little older than Eloise. Just a whole world less innocent.

'Could you, Dad?' Eloise hugged his arm in anticipation.

No trace of the weeping girl of last night. Sinclair found himself wavering. He wanted Eloise to be happy. Of late, he seemed to have lost the ability to make her so.

He remained silent but Eloise could read him too well, planting a kiss on his cheek as she cried, 'Thanks, Dad. I'm going to dress.'

She was out of the room before he could call her back. He was left with Tiree who was studying him curiously as if she could see the cracks.

'I didn't agree,' he growled at her.

'No, you didn't,' she confirmed, 'although I'm pretty sure it was you I saw dangling off her little finger.'

The comment surprised him. 'You think I'm too soft?'

'Possibly,' she replied, 'although I can see you'd want to compensate.'

Compensate for what? the words formed in Sinclair's brain but fortunately he didn't voice them aloud. Otherwise she just might tell him. He didn't need the Lousy Father of the Year award presented by her. Suspecting he was in line for it was bad enough.

'Anyway, it's up to you,' she continued, 'but I will take care of her properly.'

Tiree looked at him straight. The choice was his: either he trusted her or he didn't.

Sinclair found himself nodding and only later, sitting in Rhys's car, tried to analyse why. The conference wasn't that important. He could have said no to Eloise. He could have called up Mrs Enderby. Instead he'd entrusted his daughter to Ti Nemo, of all people.

'I'm sure they'll be fine.' Rhys sensed his mood. 'Tiree seems a great girl.'

'Mm.' Sinclair had already gathered his friend's opinion of Tiree.

Having finally gone to shave, he'd returned to the kitchen to discover a definite rapport established between the two. She certainly never laughed like that in his presence.

Refusing coffee, he had breathed disapproval on them both and, placing some spending cash on the table, limited himself to a stiff goodbye.

He could swear she'd muttered, 'Pompous,' under her breath as he'd walked away.

Not loud enough for him to be absolutely certain but Rhys had been struggling with a smile as they left the house.

'Quite a package, in fact,' Rhys continued on the same theme as they sped northwards.

'Who?' Sinclair responded unhelpfully.

'Tiree—' Rhys wasn't to be deflected '—or Miss Macleod as you insist on calling her.'

'What's wrong with that?'

'Nothing, if you want to turn back the clock half a century. I thought I'd stepped into an episode of *Upstairs, Downstairs*.'

Rhys laughed at his small joke while Sinclair merely grimaced, 'Very funny.'

'Seriously though,' Rhys resumed, 'she's really something: beautiful face, nice body *and* brains.'

Sinclair, who had been slower in appreciating Tiree, found himself irritated by Rhys's instant attraction.

'I thought you favoured busty blondes with big hair and no intellect,' he replied rather heavily.

Rhys feigned hurt. 'I do date other types of women, you know, and, even if I didn't, I'd make an exception for your Miss Macleod.'

'She's not *my* anything,' Sinclair ground back. 'She's also a girl, not a woman.'

Rhys grinned. 'Too young for me, you mean?'

Sinclair refrained from answering but his face was expressive enough.

'You're so uptight about some things, Sinc,' Rhys scoffed. 'Don't you ever feel like giving yourself a break?'

Such criticism from Rhys was hardly new. Normally Sinclair would have ignored it. No one took Rhys very seriously—least of all Rhys himself.

But it triggered off a memory of when he'd first woken. He had been dreaming, something faintly erotic judging by how easily fantasy and reality merged before he'd become conscious of who the girl in his bed was. It hadn't stopped him kissing her. Arguably he'd given himself a break then.

He acknowledged his own hypocrisy in warning Rhys off. He hadn't cared how old she was this morning, just how sweet her mouth tasted and how soft her breast felt in the palm of his hand.

'Sinc?' Rhys's voice dragged him back to the present.

'Yes?'

'I haven't given offence, have I?'

'No more than usual,' Sinclair returned drily.

'I just feel you're in danger of living to work,' Rhys ventured, 'rather than working to live. For instance, has there been anyone since Stephanie what's-her-name?'

Sinclair remaincd tight-lipped at the question.

'I'll take that as a no,' Rhys concluded, 'and that was six months ago.'

Sinclair didn't need Rhys to tell him that. 'We don't all operate a revolving-door policy, you know,' he jibed in return.

Rhys laughed unashamedly. 'Don't knock it. Regular sex is a great reliever of stress.'

'Thank you, Dr Ruth,' Sinclair grated back, 'but I'd prefer not to discuss my sex life, if it's all the same to you.'

'You have one, then?' Rhys couldn't resist asking.

It drew a threatening look from Sinclair and the suggestion, 'Why don't you just shut up and drive?'

Fortunately Rhys took the hint at last but he was still smiling as he switched on the radio.

Welcoming the end of the interrogation, Sinclair turned his attention to his speech. He'd written it weeks earlier. Just as well because, between the inquest and his meeting with Ti Nemo, his concentration was shattered. The words were his—a study of the re-emergence of TB as a source of fatality among infants—but they held little meaning or interest for him.

He was still preoccupied with his stepson's death. He needed to know the truth. What had made Kit reckless enough to overtake on a blind bend at ninety?

He was sure the key was Ti Nemo. He'd already suspected that Kit had been obsessed with her and, having now met her, he understood the attraction better.

It wasn't just physical. She exuded an odd sort of charm. Even when you didn't like her, she got under your skin, made you a little crazy.

Was that what she'd done to Kit?

CHAPTER SEVEN

TIREE was waiting by the drawing room window when the men were due to return. She'd enjoyed the day. The shops weren't too busy, Eloise proved good company and no one had approached her with the dreaded words 'aren't you...?' But, at unguarded moments, her thoughts would keep slipping back to Ewan Sinclair and their brief encounter in his bed.

She'd worked out his motivation. He was a man, not unused to the company of women if Eloise's story was true. He'd woken up, found himself next to a warm body, and allowed instinct to take over. She didn't flatter herself. It wasn't personal. She was nobody to him. Less than nobody from the way he looked at her sometimes.

The real mystery was her own reaction. She'd reached the age of twenty-three without experiencing any of the mad passion written about in songs and books. Now this. It was unbelievable. At the worst time in the most awkward situation with the least likely person, she had finally felt it: the trembling in her limbs, the heart racing, that first sweet ache of desire. No matter that she'd been too paralysed to respond.

By late afternoon she'd ceased trying to make sense of it and was now focused on not repeating such insanity. Hence her vigil at this window, counting down the minutes until the men reappeared.

When the gates finally swung open, she was ready, racing out to the forecourt to greet them.

As she approached, Rhys slid down his window. 'How are you?'

'Fine.' She returned his smile, ignoring the scowl directed at her by Sinclair from the passenger seat.

'Where's Eloise?' he asked as if he suspected her of losing his daughter somewhere.

Tiree held in a sigh. 'She's upstairs, listening to CDs.'

96

'Right.' He scarcely seemed better pleased and Tiree wondered what crime she was meant to have committed now.

He climbed out of the car and reached into the back for his briefcase.

Tiree quickly took her chance with the other man. 'Mr Williams—'

'*Rhys*, please,' he insisted.

'Rhys,' she cchoed, 'I have to go home tonight and I was hoping you could drop me off somewhere I might hire a taxi.'

'No problem. In fact, I could give you a lift home,' he volunteered almost instantly. 'Where do you live?'

'Nowhere near you,' was supplied by Sinclair, now at her shoulder, 'and don't you have a dinner date?'

'Nothing that can't be broken.' Rhys beamed another smile at Tiree.

Her heart sank. Sinclair, breathing disapproval down her neck, didn't worry her. She just hadn't figured his friend would really be interested in her.

'We could have dinner on the way,' he ran on, confirming it.

'I…um…that's kind of you but—' she sought a polite turndown.

Sinclair didn't bother with polite. His '*Rhys*!' verged on intimidating.

'Yes?' Rhys raised a brow.

'Get lost!' Sinclair told him curtly.

Rhys took it surprisingly well, lifting his shoulders and giving Tiree an apologetic grin before putting his gear stick in reverse and executing a quick turn.

'Dog in the manger,' were his last words to Sinclair, as he pulled away and waved a hand out of the window.

Tiree folded her arms and watched her means of escape disappearing through the automatic gates.

Beside her, Sinclair used a remote device to click them shut, before muttering, 'You didn't have to ask Rhys. I'll take you home if that's what you want.'

'I imagined it would be easier,' Tiree reasoned, 'and your friend didn't mind.'

'Obviously,' he said in a tone that made her wheel round to confront him.

She was expecting to see contempt on his face but it was something more subtle. Perhaps it was just weariness. With his tie pulled down and open top button, he looked like a man who'd had a long day.

'It was just a lift I wanted,' she stressed.

'I doubt the same could be said for Rhys,' he countered.

Unable to dispute this, Tiree wondered aloud, 'So what were you doing: protecting him from me or me from him?'

'Neither,' he denied, before admitting stiffly, 'perhaps I was just jealous.'

A joke, Tiree assumed, and laughed accordingly.

He did not laugh back.

'That's absurd,' she said at length.

'Yes, isn't it,' he agreed.

Tiree raised her eyes to his, wondering what game were they playing now? He answered her with a steady stare that said no game. Just the way things were.

Wrong place. Wrong time. And, most of all, wrong person. But it made no difference.

They stood there, held by a force of sexual attraction that neither could explain. Tiree felt so strung out by it, she would probably have run if he'd tried to touch her.

Instead Sinclair let his eyes wander from a face that seemed prettier each time he saw her to the body on which Rhys had commented as they'd driven up to the house. He should be used to Rhys checking women out by now, but on this occasion his friend's remark of 'nice breasts' had made his hackles rise.

No dispute. They were nice. Nice everything, in fact: per breasts, slim waist, slightly rounded hips, shapely legs encased in tight jeans. A perfect study in female anatomy. He just didn' want Rhys noticing.

Tiree barely knew how to react as Ewan Sinclair, MD, undressed her with his eyes. Nothing cool or clinical about it. Part of her wanted to protest, only she was already blushing with something closer to pleasure. What was happening to her?

He raised his head again but this time she wouldn't meet his gaze and, afraid to expose her feelings further, she fled towards the house.

Sinclair watched her walk away in what he took to be temper. He didn't blame her. Rather late, he realised how obvious his thoughts must have been.

Maybe Rhys was right: he was badly in need of a love life. Why else would he be lusting after someone so patently *un*right for him?

He followed her inside, with the idea of retrieving the situation, and tracked her down to the kitchen. She was sitting at the table, slicing vegetables on a plastic chopping board. She spared him the barest of glances before continuing to attack a courgette.

He couldn't think of anything to say that wouldn't sound odd. How did one apologise for staring at a woman's breasts? Difficult.

'Do you want some help?' he asked, realising she was cooking for the household again.

Tiree was surprised by the offer but grasped at this attempt to restore normality.

'Perhaps you could slice the chicken for the stir-fry.' She indicated the tray of meat.

He nodded and, getting another knife from a drawer, sat down to the task. 'How's your head today?'

'Fine.'

'And your ankle? I was thinking perhaps you should have rested it today.'

'It's okay, apart from the occasional twinge,' she shrugged. 'I had lots of chances to sit, anyway, while Eloise tried things on.'

'How was she?'

'Great,' Tiree assured. 'Nothing like a little retail therapy. I've spent all your money, by the way.'

'I meant you to,' he responded.

'We had lunch in town, and Eloise bought some new clothes.'

'What sort of clothes?'

'Don't worry—' Tiree read his interest correctly '—nothing on the blonde-tart line.'

Sinclair recognised the words as his from yesterday. Was she storing up all his offences?

'Look, can we start again?' he found himself appealing.

Tiree stopped chopping mid-carrot and composed herself sufficiently to give him a cool stare.

'I wasn't suggesting you'd encourage Eloise to buy anything inappropriate,' he continued. 'I just know what she's inclined to want. In fact, we've had some royal battles on the subject.'

'I wouldn't take it too seriously,' she advised. 'Chances are she's just trying to wind you up.'

'Wind me up?' he echoed.

Tiree didn't know whether it was the phrase he didn't understand or the psychology. 'She picks something sexy and outrageous to test your reaction. You go ballistic, thereby proving your total unreasonableness and allowing her to indulge in a massive sulk which ultimately means she wins.'

'You certainly have the scenario down,' Sinclair conceded, 'but how does she win?'

'Teenagers have enough spare time to sulk for Britain,' Tiree pointed out, 'but presumably you don't, so you end up cajoling-stroke-bribing her out of it.'

About to deny it, Sinclair reflected on the last year or so. He had several times had to negotiate Eloise out of her bedroom with various concessions.

'And the alternative is?' he drawled back.

Tiree shrugged. 'I don't know—maybe avoid the battle areas in the first place.'

'Let her dress how she likes?' He was clearly horrified by the idea.

'You could try it,' Tiree nodded. 'So maybe she does buy gold lamé and a micro skirt, but it's hardly the first step to her moral downfall... That's more about confidence than clothes.'

'You've lost me,' Sinclair admitted.

Tiree decided to be more direct. 'You're frightened she's going to start sleeping around at far too young an age. Right?'

'Right.' Sinclair was unsure whether he found Tiree's frankness refreshing or disturbing.

Tiree, however, had no problem talking about sex, just doing it.

'Well, short of locking her away in her room for the next five years,' she ran on, 'you won't be able to control that aspect of her life. It's going to be up to her whether she withstands the pressure.'

'From boys?'

'And girlfriends—asking whether she's done it yet, making her feel she's not one of the crowd until she has. It's not easy for girls these days.'

'Yes, well, I appreciate the advice,' he replied politely enough, 'but this is part and parcel of why I sent her to boarding school.'

Tiree gave him a look asking if he really was that naïve. 'And you imagine *what*? That posh kids don't do it because they come from homes with a bit of money?'

'Not exactly.' Sinclair wished he hadn't started this argument because he had a feeling he was going to lose it. 'But there was certainly few opportunities to mix with the opposite sex when I went to boarding school.'

'And this was which century?' she retorted flippantly.

Sinclair compressed his lips: he wasn't that ancient. 'I understand things have changed somewhat…'

'*Somewhat*?' Tiree raised a brow. 'It's a different world to your day or even mine. Ask Eloise if you don't believe me.'

'Ask her what precisely?' Sinclair was struggling to keep the pompous tone out of his voice.

'Whether the girls talk much about boys?' Tiree suggested. 'Do they read teen mags? Have any of them claimed to have done the deed? What does Eloise herself think about casual sex?'

'I can't ask her those things!' he protested with an appalled expression.

'Why not?' Tiree demanded in reply. 'Who else can she talk to?'

Up till then, it hadn't occurred to Sinclair his daughter needed a forum for such discussion.

'There's a matron and a house-mistress at Wesley Hall,' he pointed out, on the defensive.

Tiree rolled her eyes. 'I imagine the girls would die rather than talk sex with either of them.'

She could be right. Sinclair admitted that. She just didn't have to sound so cocksure.

He found himself scowling back, 'Sex isn't the only thing in life, you know!'

Tiree had to agree. It was conspicuous in its absence from hers, for a start. But coming from him—Mr I may not like you but I am prepared to bed you—it was a bit rich.

'Oh, *I* know,' she replied with emphasis before deciding the conversation was better ended.

She pushed back her chair and, picking up the sliced vegetables and chicken, crossed to the hob to light the burners under two heavy-based frying pans.

Sinclair was left to appreciate his own absurdity. Had he really tried to adopt the moral high ground when, even now, a desire to strangle this girl warred with an equally strong desire to pull her into his arms and kiss her? The fact she must know how he felt made it worse. He was surprised she'd stopped short of calling him a hypocrite. That said, he was surprised by her generally.

Tiree was aware of him watching her as she stir-fried the food. She supposed she was a curiosity to him. They came from very different worlds.

She broke the silence, only when the meal was ready. 'You'd better call Eloise.'

'Okay.' He walked out into the hall and shouted upstairs before reappearing to ask, 'White or red wine?'

'White, please.' Tiree hoped a glass might relax her.

'Dry or sweet?'

'Dry.'

He selected a bottle from those chilling in the fridge and was opening it when Eloise sauntered into the kitchen, wearing one of her new outfits.

'Hi, Dad,' Eloise was still in cheery spirits. 'How did the conference go?'

'Deathly dull,' he replied, 'apart from my lecture, of course.'

'Of course.' Eloise echoed her father's wry tone. 'We had great fun. Tiree helped me buy some new gear.'

'So I see.' Sinclair's gaze rested momentarily on his daughter, looking tall and leggy and suddenly much older in a short blue skirt and a white T-shirt emblazoned with the words 'Men Lie'. He was still deciding whether he liked it when he felt Tiree's eyes boring into him, warning him to say the right thing. 'Very…um…cool?'

'Cool?' Eloise had never heard her father use that word before. 'You really think so?'

'Sure.' He smiled at her. 'Although I'll try not to take the logo too personally.'

'*Men lie*,' Eloise read the slogan with a grin. 'That doesn't mean you, Dad. It's about men men.'

'Right.' Sinclair had a feeling he was being insulted. The smile flitting across Tiree's face seemed to confirm it.

Meanwhile Eloise transferred her attention to the food Tiree had laid on the table. 'Stir-fry, wicked!'

'Help yourselves.' Tiree balked at serving up; she wasn't applying for the position of housekeeper, after all.

She'd cooked the chicken and vegetables in separate frying pans and spooned a mixture of peppers, mushrooms, celery and baby sweetcorn on her own plate.

Eloise noticed that she avoided the meat. 'Don't you like chicken?'

'I'm vegetarian,' explained Tiree.

'I am almost, too,' Eloise claimed while heaping chicken onto her plate.

'Since when?' her father enquired with raised brow.

'Since I ate the school's mince.' Eloise made a gagging gesture. 'I think they do it deliberately. Make the food so bad it saves money because no one wants to eat it.'

'An interesting theory,' Sinclair drawled. 'Perhaps I'll put it to Miss Hesslewaite when I drive you back.'

He was obviously joking as Eloise recognised with her,

'Very funny, Dad,' but some of her good spirits evaporated at mention of her imminent return. 'Dad thinks disgusting food and lumpy beds are character building. What do you think?'

'I think I'll stay out of this,' Tiree answered pleasantly enough.

But Eloise, hoping for support, added, 'I bet your parents didn't send you to boarding school.'

Tiree shook her head. 'No, they didn't. I went to a private day-school.'

Sinclair raised a brow at this information. Weren't her parents dead and absent, respectively?

Tiree caught his sceptical look from across the table. It was ironic. While she'd told him the truth, she often ducked it with other people as she had just now with Eloise.

She'd found in the past that her life story tended to attract an unpleasant blend of pity and curiosity. Poor thing, abandoned at birth. What were you wearing? Was there a note? How old were you? Etc. Etc. Questions Tiree was tired of answering.

She'd known from the outset she wouldn't get that treatment from Dr Bedside Mannerless, now regarding her with his best cynical, clinical expression.

She stared right back at him, daring him to call her a liar.

'Your parents sent you to this private school?' he finally challenged.

'Foster-parents,' she relayed matter-of-factly.

'You were in care?'

'Yes.'

'They must have been fond of you, these foster-parents,' Sinclair ventured, still with that sceptical air, 'to have paid for your education.'

'You don't know how fond.' And Tiree wasn't about to tell him.

'What about the commune?' he queried the inconsistencies in her story.

Tiree gave a shrug rather than answer. If he wanted her autobiography, he'd have to wait and buy a copy.

'What's a commune?' Eloise reminded them of her presence.

'Nothing important,' Sinclair dismissed and returned to the original subject. 'It's your schooling that's the issue. And, believe me, there are many, less fortunate children who'd consider a boarding school with swimming pool, tennis courts and cinema a dream come true rather than hell on earth.'

Tiree realised what he was saying: count your blessings. But children of Eloise's age rarely did. They were too focused on the here and now and their own private hang-ups.

Eloise's face formed a sullen mask before she came back with, 'I tell you what, Dad, why don't you go out and find one and offer them my place, seeing I'm so ungrateful?'

'Eloise—' he was visibly counting to ten '—if that's meant to be funny—'

'It isn't,' Eloise scowled back, 'and neither's boarding school. Not that I expect you to understand.'

'I understand better than you imagine,' Sinclair countered. 'I was eight when I went to Prep School, and, yes, I remember being fairly miserable for a time, but it will get better. You just have to give it a chance.'

'A chance?' Eloise rolled her eyes. 'What do you call ten months? The worst ten months of my life!'

'Don't exaggerate!' her father snapped back.

'I'm not!' Eloise's voice was rising in temper.

'Um, excuse me,' Tiree stepped in smartly, 'but one aspect of family life I don't feel like reliving is rows over the dinner table, so if you could postpone this one till I'm gone, I'd be grateful.'

Tiree meant it. Their quarrelling seemed pointless. They'd obviously been round this territory countless times and arrived nowhere.

The intervention effectively called time out as father and daughter switched their attention to Tiree who, having delivered these words of wisdom, went back to eating.

Sinclair considered indignation but decided against it. The girl had a point, if a fairly irritating way of putting it. Why was he quarrelling with Eloise in front of a virtual stranger?

He caught his daughter's eye and they exchanged looks agreeing a truce.

Then he broke the silence with an intentionally mundane, 'Would you like more wine?'

'Please.' Tiree held out her glass, and, happy to move the conversation along, directed at Eloise, 'What's it like, the CD you bought?'

'Great.' Eloise seized eagerly on the subject. 'Even better than their last one... Tiree knows lots about music,' she told her father. 'She used to work in a music shop.'

'Really?'

'A long time ago, when I was a student.'

'A girl of many parts,' he commented.

More disbelief but Tiree chose to ignore it.

Eloise couldn't quite read the undercurrents, but said, 'The only music Dad likes is the boring stuff by dead people.'

Sinclair's mouth quirked. 'That's one way of summing up the great composers... I don't imagine you're a classical fan, either.'

Why not? Tiree wondered. Did he think her not intellectual enough to appreciate more complex music?

'Depends what it is. I like listening to Beethoven, Verdi, some Mahler, but I prefer playing Ravel and Vivaldi.'

'Playing?' he echoed. 'An instrument, you mean?'

'Violin,' she volunteered.

'Hence Rhys's reference this morning,' he concluded for himself. 'How well do you play?'

'I can pick out a tune.' Tiree resisted telling him that she'd studied at the Royal Academy in Glasgow. It would lay her open to other questions and she doubted he would believe the answers.

'That's a coincidence.' His eyes narrowed in challenge. 'Eloise was learning the violin for a while. I'm sure we still have her instrument. Perhaps you could perform for us later.'

He was trying to put her on the spot, but Tiree was happy to call his bluff. 'Sure, why not?'

Eloise glanced from one face to the other, aware there was some subtext to this conversation. 'I'll go get it now, if you want.'

Neither of the adults responded for a moment. Sinclair's eyes remained on Tiree, waiting for her to come up with some excuse. She smiled back with insouciance.

Sinclair was the one to eventually reply, 'No, finish your meal first, Eloise.'

'In case I put you off with my playing, he means,' Tiree added cheekily.

Eloise subsided in her chair. 'You can't be worse than me. Even *I* didn't like the sound... I'd have preferred to learn the guitar but Dad's frightened I'll want to run away and join a rock band like Kit.'

If it was a joke, Sinclair didn't look very amused.

'No, I'm not,' he denied but not very convincingly.

'Not that I'd ever be able to play like him.' Eloise's eyes filled up a little. 'He was brilliant.'

'Yes, he was,' Tiree agreed without thinking.

'You've heard him?' Eloise was pleased at the idea.

Tiree admitted circumspectly, 'A few times, yes.'

'You're lucky. I wanted to go and see him in concert but I was too young,' Eloise ran on. 'I've got all his CDs, though... Maybe you'd like to listen to some later?'

Tiree's gaze shifted between the girl's hopeful expression and the warning look on Sinclair's face; rather like walking through a minefield, this dinner was turning out to be.

'That would be cool,' she finally said to the girl, 'but I'm afraid I'll have to be heading home soon.'

'Can't you stay another night?' Eloise implored. 'It's Saturday tomorrow. You won't be taking me back to school until Sunday, will you?' she pleaded of her father.

'We'll see,' Sinclair answered. 'For now, if you've finished your meal, I suggest you go upstairs and write a letter of apology to Miss Hesslewaite for absconding.'

Eloise pulled a face. 'Oh, Dad, do I have to? She's going to be horrible to me, either way.'

'It's the least you can do,' Sinclair's tone made it an order, 'considering the trouble you've caused. And, afterwards, straight to bed.'

'Oh, Dad.' She rolled her eyes and appealed to Tiree, 'Could you do me a favour and make my father realise I'm not six anymore?'

'I'll do my best.' Tiree returned the girl's departing grin, and, ignoring Sinclair's stony look, obliged, 'She's not six any more.'

'Believe me, I'm well aware of that, but she's not eighteen, either.'

'She *will* be.'

'Meaning?'

Sinclair arched a brow in challenge but Tiree chose to duck this particular issue. 'Nothing.'

'Not about to impart another pearl of wisdom,' he drawled on, '*vis-à-vis* teenage girls, the rearing of?'

'If that's a dig about the advice I gave you earlier,' Tiree bristled at this sarcasm, 'I wasn't setting myself up as some kind of expert.'

'No?' He feigned disappointment. 'And there was I, thinking child psychology might be another of the many strings to your bow.'

This was, of course, a snide reference to the violin which he almost certainly doubted she played. But if he imagined he could belittle her, he was very much mistaken.

'Actually, I have no college qualifications and few school ones, either, so you feel as superior as you want, *Doctor* Sinclair, if that's what does it for you,' she threw back. 'Meanwhile, you won't object if I use your telephone to call myself a taxi.'

She rose from the table, dignity intact, and walked towards the door.

'Look, Tiree—' he tried to call her back, but she turned a deaf ear.

Sinclair swore under his breath and promised himself he wasn't going to pursue her this time. Let her disappear in the night. He sure as hell didn't need the grief.

He should have had her leave with Rhys. They'd probably make a good pair. Rhys wouldn't care that the girl was a serial liar, just so long as he got her into bed. And the girl was probably well used to such transient relationships. All too easily he could picture them together.

The only problem was the image drove him more than a little crazy.

CHAPTER EIGHT

TIREE was congratulating herself on irritating him so much he didn't follow when he suddenly appeared in the study doorway. She continued to scan through the copy of Yellow Pages she'd found on his desk.

'What are you looking for?'

'Taxi firms.'

She selected one at random and lifted the receiver. She had pushed five numbers before he crossed to her side and put out a finger to disconnect the line.

'I thought you had no money.'

'I have at the cottage.'

Tiree waited for him to remove his finger. Instead he took the receiver from her hand and placed it back on its hook.

He loomed over her, his face grim and determined, but Tiree wasn't unduly frightened. He couldn't keep her here against her will.

'This is silly,' she muttered. 'I can just go down to the village and call from there.'

'I said I'd take you home,' he responded, 'and I will, but you'd better read the evening paper first. Wait here till I fetch it.'

He walked out into the hall. She heard the unclick of a briefcase. He returned with a crumpled newspaper and locked the study door behind him.

The move made Tiree understandably nervous. 'What are you doing?'

'Making sure Eloise doesn't barge in,' he told her in clipped tones before he flattened the newspaper on the desk before her. 'I bought this at a petrol station. Not my usual read but it caught the eye.'

Tiree's heart sank. It wasn't in banner headlines; that honour had gone to the proposed underground strike. Nevertheless she'd made front page.

A small photograph—a grainy blow-up of one snapped on leaving the private hospital yesterday—was accompanied by the byline: *Is this the real face of Ti Nemo, wild girl of rock?*

She groaned aloud before leafing to the main article on page four. She sank down on a chair as she read about her brief stay at the Abbey and her subsequent disappearance. Typically the Press had got it wrong, suggesting she'd been admitted to the hospital after suffering a nervous collapse. Her manager, Leslie Gray, denied any knowledge of her current whereabouts, fuelling speculation that she'd now gone missing. Meanwhile Kinetic Sugar's last single was set for another week at number one.

'I thought you'd telephoned your manager,' Sinclair said when she pushed the newspaper away in disgust.

'I have,' Tiree reaffirmed. 'He's just milking the situation to hype record sales.'

'Which must suit you in turn,' Sinclair mused aloud.

'I'm not party to this,' Tiree insisted angrily. 'Don't you understand? This photo could cost me any chance of a normal life.'

Sinclair almost laughed at the notion of Ti Nemo leading a normal life. Who was she kidding?

'A good launch pad for a solo career, though,' he speculated.

Tiree shook her head, wearying of his cynicism, and picked up the newspaper once more. 'Would you recognise me from this?'

She raised her face and Sinclair scrutinised each feature: wide, slanting green eyes, neat nose, lips with a natural pout and a slightly pointed chin. The newspaper picture hardly did her justice.

He found himself staring overlong and shifted his gaze away. 'Not instantly, but it's not unlike you when you're scowling.'

'Great. I'll just have to go around grinning like an idiot for the rest of my life.' Despondent, she finished reading the whole article which included more details about the Abbey. Apparently it wasn't any run-of-the-mill private hospital. 'It says here that the Abbey specialises in psychological disorders resulting from head injury. Is that true?'

He nodded briefly.

'But if I had a simple concussion,' she queried, 'why did I end up there?'

'The ambulance crew took you to the Abbey under my instruction,' he admitted. 'It was the nearest hospital to your cottage and I knew it was equipped to deal with head trauma. I also believed the staff would be more likely to be discreet than a normal casualty department.'

He'd certainly miscalculated on that score. 'Wonderful, so now the world thinks I've had a breakdown,' she sighed heavily.

'I thought I was acting in your best interests,' he stated stiffly, 'but, yes, I see now it may not have been the right choice.'

Was that an apology? It certainly came close, and Tiree unbent a little in response.

'You weren't to know,' she conceded, 'and I suppose I should be grateful you didn't just decide to leave me for someone else to find.'

'I wouldn't have done that,' he replied in grave tones.

'No.' Tiree realised that Ewan Sinclair, the man as well as the doctor, lived by a code of ethics.

'I could get Bob—Dr Chivers—to issue a disclaimer, stating you were admitted solely on the grounds of a head injury,' he suggested.

Tiree considered the offer for a moment or two, before shaking her head. 'Forget it. Disclaimers to the Press tend to backfire... Here, you'd better destroy this so Eloise won't see it.'

She handed him back the newspaper and watched as he ripped out the offending pages, tore them into little pieces, then deposited the lot in a bin.

'Thanks for keeping quiet to Eloise, by the way,' he remarked.

'What else was I going to do,' Tiree shrugged. 'Tell her who I was so she could spit in my eye? I assume you've shared your opinions as to my part in Kit's death.'

'How could I do that? I don't know what part you played.'
He was staring at her again, waiting for what—a full and frank confession?

It was as if the last couple of days hadn't happened. He'd rescued her from the fall, helped her evade the Press, given her a bed for the night and even indulged a passing desire with a kiss or two. But nothing had changed: he still believed her responsible in some way for Kit's accident.

She rose from the desk, driven more by anger than guilt, and tried to slip past him, only to find her arm caught in a firm grip. She didn't struggle but adopted a look of boredom.

Sinclair made her an offer. 'If you were to tell me what really happened that night, it won't go further than these walls.'

'Like I can trust you?' she threw back.

'You can trust the fact that I wouldn't want any publicity, touching me and mine,' he rejoined. 'I'll settle for truth rather than retribution.'

Tiree tried to draw away from him and he tightened his hold, hurting whether he meant to or not.

'All right—' she would give him the confession he sought '—I was responsible. I knew Kit was too hyped up to be safe on the bike. I could have stopped him leaving if I'd wanted. Instead Stu chased after him and they crashed. End of story... Happy?'

'No,' he grated back, 'you still haven't told it all.'

What did he want—blood?

Probably.

'Isn't it enough that I've taken the blame?' she retorted.

Apparently not, as he pursued, 'How could you have stopped Kit?'

She rolled her eyes. 'Him male. Me female. Do you need a diagram?'

'Not now, no.' It confirmed Sinclair's suspicions—that she'd been having a relationship with his stepson—but he felt no better for knowing. In fact, he felt a great deal worse. 'So why reject him that night? Grown tired of him, had we?'

'Not the way you mean,' Tiree denied. 'I was tired, full stop.'

'Swapping between the two of them,' his mouth formed a sneer, 'I imagine you were.'

Tiree made a sound of frustration. Did he really see her as a *femme fatale*?

'You couldn't be more wrong!'

'Then tell me!'

Tiree looked up at a face that could have been carved in granite. No feeling, no understanding, no way would she expose her real flaws to him. She'd sooner he believed her a heartless tart.

'You're right,' she hurled back. 'Only why limit it to Stu and Kit? Maybe I was involved with Wayne, the drummer, too. And there's Les, of course, our manager, not to mention all the roadies in the crew. Maybe I go with every man I meet... Who knows, if you weren't such a pompous, self-righteous prig, perhaps I might even sleep with you!'

Sinclair realised her words were intended to ridicule and he growled in response, 'You think I'd sleep with you?'

'Given half a chance, yeah!' Tiree was spurred on by those superior English tones.

She cocked her head at a defiant angle, inviting him to repudiate it. She was so sure he would, convinced his pride would have him push her away.

It seemed she'd read him well. He released her arm as if he feared contamination. She allowed herself a satisfied smile.

Too soon and too obvious, it was a definite mistake.

When she tried to walk away, hands were suddenly clamped on her waist. 'Maybe you're right.'

'W-what are you doing?' she stammered as he drew her against his body.

The mocking look was now on *his* face, savouring her panic. 'Living down to your expectations.'

'Let me go!' Tiree jerked backwards and placed flattened palms on his chest.

It was as pointless as pushing against a brick wall. Taller and stronger, he was determined to teach her a lesson.

And today's lesson turned out to be about weakness. Hers. Taught with consummate ease as he gathered her closer, inch ing his head towards hers and, instead of dread, a shiver of anticipation worked its way up her spine.

Perhaps if he'd been rough, she would have fought harder, but he wasn't. The kiss was gentle, a bare touch at first, a stir of breath against her cheek, then the warm press of a firm male mouth. He took it slowly, drawing out this sweet assault, pulling on her top lip, then her bottom lip until she gave an involuntary moan of submission.

It should have been enough to make a point, but Sinclair found he wanted more, wanted it all. He thrust a hand in her hair and held her head steady as he deepened the kiss, demanding a response.

Tiree gasped, allowing him entry. His tongue slid inside her mouth, a weapon of intimacy as he began to taste her. She waited for the usual revulsion and instead felt a kick of desire in her belly so strong she moaned aloud.

A hand pushed up under her T-shirt. Fingers spread against her ribcage, smoothing over skin, seeking what he had touched that morning. She caught at his arm.

He groaned against her mouth, 'Let me…'

She whimpered in response. It could have meant anything. He chose to believe it meant yes.

The hand slid upwards, encountering no barrier. He cupped a breast in his palm. It was as soft and full as he remembered, the aureoles large. He tried to imagine her naked, but imagining wasn't enough. He stopped kissing her and drew away.

Tiree almost protested. Was that it? Over?

But no. He held her eyes for a moment, then, not waiting for permission, pulled the T-shirt over her head. He dropped it on the floor and looked at her again, long and hard.

When Tiree might have covered herself, he breathed the word, 'Beautiful,' and lifted a hand to her breast.

Tiree meant to resist. She shut her eyes against the sight of his handsome, unsmiling face, but, if anything, it was more acute, the blind sensation of skin on bare skin, moulding, softly stroking, reverent at first, then skilful, thumb and forefinger teasing, pulling, making the bud swell and swell.

She trusted that desire would eventually die away, only it

went on growing as he began to fondle her other breast. Wa:
that her moaning? No, it couldn't be, making those sexy, plead
ing noises, her head falling back as she let him touch her. Wa
this what it was all about, wanting someone so badly nothing
else mattered?

He lifted her onto the desk, pushing aside papers and book
before he lay her back on the leather top and put his mouth t
her swollen flesh. She opened her eyes and watched Ewar
Sinclair nuzzling at her breast. He seemed what he was—:
stranger to her—yet still she craved this. She put her hands t
his dark head and held him there, urging him on as he sucke
and licked and ultimately bit on the nipple until it stood prou
and hurting, and left the other aching for the same rough lov
ing. She pushed it towards him and he groaned in satisfactio
as he took it in his mouth.

More books were falling with soft thuds onto the carpete
floor as he half climbed onto the desk beside her. His breat
was coming thick and fast like her own. He placed his han
on the flat of her stomach, and undid the stud button and zi
of her jeans. He started to push the material from her hips.

Only then did she feel the familiar panic and grabbed at hi
arm but it was too late. He was inside her pants, reachin
downwards between her thighs, stroking her with a slow han
until she had no desire for him to stop. Her legs fell open t
let skilful fingers slip inside her. She was already warm an
wet at the first thrust, moaning at the next, sliding her hand
over the sweat sheen on his body to hold him there.

He was kissing her again, mouth hungry this time, invading
demanding. She was tasting him, too, accepting the intimac
from which she normally cringed, grasping handfuls of his ha
as fingers entered deeper and deeper, making her want mor
of him—all of him—inside her.

She reached for him, and swallowed hard as she felt th
pulse of his manhood. It strained at his clothes, pushed again:
her hand.

Sinclair drew away from her, urging, 'Wait.'

He moved to the edge of the desk, taking her with hin
dropping her feet back to the floor so he could push down he

jeans. She might have protested but his mouth was back on hers. She might have resisted but his hand was sliding between her thighs, a fist kneading her flesh until she was whimpering for him again. Then he was lifting her back on the desk, dragging off her jeans before coming to stand between her thighs.

He stopped kissing and touching her for a moment and Tiree opened her eyes to see him stripping off his own shirt. Just looking at him aroused her. But it confused her, too—to feel this way for a man she barely liked.

Sinclair caught her gaze and saw the doubts in it. She began to shake her head but he obeyed his own urges. He reached for her breasts again, so full and round, putting his mouth to one engorged nipple, circling it with his tongue, sucking until he drew a gasp. He nuzzled the other. A hand pushed into his hair to hold him there. He sensed her yielding to him and couldn't wait any longer.

Tiree felt his hands on her hips, dragging her nearer, then his flesh pushing against hers, the shaft long and hard as he released it. Further than she'd ever been with a man, she tensed with fright. He made to enter her and, at the last moment, she tried to pull back.

But it was already too late. He was thrusting inside her, breaking more than mental barriers, and she was crying out in startled anguish as Sinclair finally grasped the truth.

He jerked his head back and stared at her with complete incredulity. 'Hell, you're a virgin!'

It was question, statement and accusation, all rolled into one, and Tiree hadn't even anticipated him noticing.

'Not any more, I don't think,' she attempted a joke.

There was an audible crack in her voice.

He rested his forehead against hers. 'Why did you…?'

Let him? Tiree shook her head. There was no point in looking to her for answers.

Sinclair was left doing battle with his own conscience. Unbelievably he was still aroused and controlling a strong urge to finish what he had started. He felt her body begin trembling with reaction. He wanted to ignore it but couldn't. He withdrew and straightened his clothes.

He finally looked at her. Her expression was blank, as if she was in shock. What the hell had he done?

'It's all right,' he murmured, aware how inadequate the words were. Nothing seemed right about this any more.

Tiree looked at him with incomprehension. Why him? Why now?

'Here.' He picked up her discarded T-shirt and, turning it the right way out, gently pulled it over her head.

Tiree wrapped her arms about her body but couldn't seem to stop shaking. She snapped out of it a little when he retrieved her underwear. She felt a blush creeping up her face and, taking the garment from him, she sidled round to the other side of the desk to tug it on.

The absurdity of the situation struck her as she did so. She'd let him take off her clothes with little fuss and here she was dying of embarrassment when he tried to put them back on.

In fact, the whole desire thing was absurd. She'd wanted this man more than she had any other yet wasn't sure if she ever liked him. He, in turn, had wanted her when he thought her a tart and couldn't retreat fast enough when he discovered she wasn't.

'Look—' he handed her her jeans next '—I can't begin to say how sorry I am.'

'Then don't.' Her usual hard front slipped back into place. 'We're both embarrassed enough as it is.'

'True.' Sinclair shrugged into his own shirt but found there were too many buttons missing to tie it.

He watched as she walked towards the armchair by the window and sat to pull on her jeans. He caught a glimpse of slim shapely legs. Desire might have been dampened but it was easily resurrected. He thought of how soft her skin was, how sweet she tasted, how sexy the little sounds she made when he gave her pleasure, and he felt a powerful urge to seduce her all over again.

He dragged his eyes away and fixed them elsewhere. He noticed the contents of his desk scattered on the floor. He bent to pick the debris up and absently sorted through some papers

Tiree saw him doing so and concluded: interlude over, back to normal.

Well, what else did she expect? A protestation of undying love? Hardly. Sex was just sex to men, as Stu had explained more than once. A big deal when it was happening. Nothing when it was over.

And that was when it ended well. Not halfway through when one of the partners had withdrawn from the game with an injury. What a fiasco!

'Tiree—' he'd finally finished his tidying and, remembering her existence, trained concerned eyes on her '—I don't really know how we should deal with this. I accept responsibility for what just happened. Of course, I do. But I don't quite understand why you…well, why you didn't stop me.'

Tiree didn't understand it, either. She had liked other men more. She was sure she had, even though she'd balked at intimacy. Yet this time desire had overwhelmed her. Perhaps it was simply a case that Ewan Sinclair, for all his stuffiness and pomposity, was just bloody good at sex!

It seemed a reasonable explanation but not one she was about to share, so she resorted to a sarcastic, 'You'll have to ask my analyst.'

'You have one?' He sounded hopeful.

'No.' Her mouth quirked. 'That was a joke.'

'I see.' Sinclair was far from laughing as he added quietly, 'I'm not a great advocate of analysis *per se*, but some people do gain benefit from it. Perhaps you should consider it.'

'Thanks.' His advice went down like a lead balloon as Tiree retorted, 'You think any woman mad enough to sleep with you is in need of psychiatric help, is that it? Well, you could be right.'

Sinclair made a face at the comment but supposed he'd asked for it. After all, his concern for her mental welfare had come rather late in the day.

'It seems I haven't been right about anything so far,' he admitted, shaking his head. 'I just need you to know that if I'd been aware that you hadn't ever been with a man, I wouldn't have touched you.'

Tiree might have been embarrassed at this sober statement had it not struck her as faintly ridiculous. 'You mean you don' fancy me any more now you realise I'm not a tart?'

'Yes…or rather no…that isn't what I meant.' Sinclair wa reminded just how impossible he found this girl. 'Nothing say is going to improve the situation, is it?' he added stiffly.

'I wouldn't think so,' Tiree agreed. 'You could pass me m sandals, however.'

'What?' Sinclair blinked at the prosaic request. 'Yes, o course.'

He bent down to locate her shoes, rescuing the left one fron under the desk. He gave them to her and watched as she slippe them on. She appeared calm and collected, which was surel strange in itself. But what did he really know about this girl Very little, it seemed.

Tiree waited for him to step back before rising from th chair. She felt a little light-headed and stood still for a momen getting her balance, then crossed to the telephone.

She couldn't remember the taxi-firm number so she opene the Yellow Pages again. She half expected him to shut the boo' on her, but, no, he remained a silent onlooker. She conclude he was now just as anxious for her to leave.

She dialled the number, unhindered. When the cab controlle asked her for her precise location, she had to elicit Sinclair' help and he gave it without demur.

'They're fairly busy but they've promised to be within th hour,' she relayed.

He nodded at the information. 'I'd offer you a lift but Elois has probably gone to bed. I don't suppose you'd accept on either.'

His tone was ponderous with guilt. Tiree raised her eyes t his face. Guilt there, too. She could have enjoyed it, twiste the knife more, but honesty compelled her to do otherwise.

After all, she hadn't exactly been screaming 'rape' whe he'd seduced her. Rather the opposite, if she remembere rightly. She certainly remembered how she'd felt and, right u to the last part, it had been good.

'Look, Sinclair—' she called him by his last name as every

one did '—you seem to be under the impression that you've done something awful to me, but it really isn't that big a deal. So if you're worrying that I'm going to freak out about it, then don't! I'm fine.'

'I'd like to believe that,' he returned quietly.

'You can,' she assured, although 'fine' was a bit of an exaggeration.

Not that she felt particularly awful, either. Just confused. Still struggling with the question: why him?

Sinclair wasn't altogether convinced but he couldn't see how he could keep her against her will. He crossed to the study door and unlocked it. He held it open while she walked past him into the hall.

'Why don't you sit in the drawing room,' he suggested, 'and I'll make us some coffee while we're waiting?'

Tiree followed his polite lead, murmuring, 'Thanks.'

He made his escape.

Entering the drawing room, Tiree bet he was breathing as big a sigh of relief as she was. Talk about awkward situations.

She crossed to a sofa by the window from which she could see the front gates. She willed the taxi to come sooner rather than later. She'd never been in a morning-after-the-night-before situation but she imagined it couldn't be much more bizarre than this one.

She wondered what Stu would have said. Something crude or funny? Probably both. Stu hadn't been much of a romantic. Sex had been more a matter of power than love to Stu. Love was for dopes.

Yet he'd loved her in his own way and she'd loved him, too. Or needed him, anyway. Maybe that was the same thing. Certainly he'd been the closest thing she had to family after the breakdown of her placement with the Chisolms.

He was the only one she told about what had happened with Tom Chisolm, and, though he'd advised her to live with it, he'd also understood her need for retribution.

She'd been back at the children's home a week when Stu had suggested they pay the Chisolms a visit. Not an official one or at a time the couple were likely to be in. They'd use a key Tiree still had in her possession and trust that the burglar alarm hadn't been changed.

Till then Tiree had been a law-abiding citizen who'd scarcely earned a detention at school, but a kind of craziness had overtaken her as she'd cut up Tom and Margaret's clothes, slashed cushions, hurled ornaments. Stu, anarchic by nature, had been happy to help her and they'd pretty much trashed the house.

They'd gone on the run afterwards. A whole month they'd survived, begging for loose change, eating in soup kitchens, sleeping in doorways. Hardly an adventure even before autumn turned into a harsh, Scottish winter. When the police finally hauled them in, Tiree had acquired a hacking cough and was almost resigned to the secure unit Stu had warned her they might face.

But no, it was just back to Sunnydale and a little lecture on the subject of dangers on the street. No criminal charges. No mention of the Chisolms, although it must have been obvious who had done over their house. They could only assume the couple hadn't reported it and Tiree hadn't felt inclined to confess.

Tiree had never tried to see the Chisolms again. She'd blanked them out as best she could, determined they wouldn't be allowed to ruin her life. Arguably they hadn't. She'd survived care and, with a measure of luck and a bit of talent, she'd gone on to fame and fortune. But Tom Chisolm's assault had messed with her head sufficiently to make normal relations with men impossible.

Well, until tonight that was, and even then, she wasn't sure what had happened with Sinclair could be called normal. She couldn't quite recall how it had begun—something she'd said, mocking him? But once started, it had seemed as unstoppable as a hurricane. Truth was she hadn't really wanted to stop it. Truth was it had been Sinclair who had called time the moment he found out she wasn't who or what he imagined.

Maybe he saw it as getting in too deep. After all, he'd simply wanted the truth and possibly retribution for Kit's death. Perhaps deflowering her was just one step too far. Whatever his thinking, he now couldn't wait to get rid of her. Obviously he hadn't appreciated the honour of being her first lover.

She might have taken offence, if she hadn't found the situation equally weird. Of all the men she'd met in her life, she couldn't have chosen anyone more unsuitable. A pompous, intellectual-type with a jaundiced view of the pop industry, he came from a background where kids like her and Stu—especially Stu—were a social phenomenon encountered solely in documentaries They weren't real people whom they'd want to invite into their homes.

Okay, so he *had* invited her but his reasons were connected to Kit and once he'd failed to prove his point—whatever that was—he couldn't wait to get shot of her. Well, she wasn't going to outstay her welcome. She had her pride.

Meanwhile he was avoiding her, Tiree reckoned. Fifteen minutes gone and no sign of that coffee. She hoped it would come soon. Her eyes were drooping. It had been a very long day.

Sinclair found her asleep, one leg on his sofa, the other on the floor. He decided not to wake her for coffee. Wait till the taxi came. That way conversation would be minimal.

After all, what was there to say? I'm sorry for stealing your innocence. No, too ridiculously old-fashioned and, at any rate, she'd made it plain she didn't want his apologies. So what did she want from him? Nothing, it seemed. Quite willing to walk out of his life for ever. So wasn't that the best thing to do—let her go?

Best for both of them, surely, Sinclair concluded as he sat there, watching her in sleep. She looked so young, her face unmarked by experience, but he knew it was an illusion. There'd been experiences—just not the kind he'd assumed. Perhaps if he'd really tried to talk to her, been more approachable, he would have discovered the truth earlier.

But would it have stopped him acting as he had? Even now, he wasn't sure.

The taxi came, the driver buzzing on the intercom. He rose and touched her shoulder. She stirred but refused to wake. He shook her a little harder and she muttered a protest, unintelligible except for the name Stu.

So that's who haunted her dreams.

He left her then and, going out to the gate, he compensated the taxi driver for a wasted journey. She was still fast asleep when he returned. He considered carrying her upstairs but feared she might wake and jump to wrong conclusions, and who could blame her? In the end, he fetched a duvet and lightly draped it over her, switching off the main lights and on a table lamp in case she was disorientated if she woke in the night.

He brushed her brow with the back of his hand, testing her temperature, only the feelings it stirred were not those of a doctor. She was cool to the touch, though the room seemed stifling. Maybe she wasn't the one with the fever.

On that fanciful note Sinclair left her.

CHAPTER NINE

As a teenager, Tiree had learned to sleep on park benches and street doorways so a warm, comfortable sofa presented no problems. Only once did she stir in the night and, having ascertained she was in safe surroundings, fell back to sleep almost immediately.

When she next hit consciousness, it was morning, and someone was standing over her, partially blocking out the sunlight streaming through opened curtains.

She blinked sleep out of her eyes, resisted asking why she was still there and opted for sarcasm instead. 'That's the longest I've ever waited for a coffee. Did you go to Brazil for the beans?'

'Very droll,' he applauded, before admitting, 'I couldn't get the percolator to work last night.'

'I would have done without,' she grimaced, even as she sat up to take a cup of the promised coffee from his hand.

'I did try and waken you,' he claimed.

Tiree believed him. Last night was coming back to her in full, Technicolor detail. She hoped she wasn't blushing but rather felt she was.

'Oh well—' she went for upbeat and casual '—I'll drink this and just go down to the village to get a taxi.'

'I'm afraid not,' he replied. 'Ours is a one-horse no-taxi town. Anyway, I'd prefer you stayed for breakfast... Eloise is counting on it.'

Eloise, not him. Well, what did she expect?

'Sure.' She shrugged her assent. 'Perhaps you could call me a taxi for later.'

He nodded briefly, then departed.

Tiree drank her coffee, scrupulously avoiding any further recollection of last night. Instead she planned the day ahead:

return to cottage, get money and passport, fly off to some far-flung country where no one had ever heard of Kinetic Sugar.

First on the agenda, however, was a shower and she took the liberty of going upstairs to the guest suite on the second floor. She had to re-wear the same clothes but at least she felt clean.

She went back downstairs to find Sinclair and Eloise in the kitchen, waiting on her arrival to begin a breakfast of juice, cereal, croissants and coffee.

Conversation flowed easily between the two females. Sinclair, however, was withdrawn. He kept looking at his watch and Tiree concluded he couldn't wait for her to be gone.

He was up out of his seat the moment he heard the sound of the buzzer, heralding someone at the gates. Tiree assumed it was her taxi but, when she would have followed, he virtually ordered her to stay.

Made to feel like a naughty dog, Tiree couldn't resist pulling a face at his retreating back.

Eloise grinned in complicity.

Then Tiree subsided on her chair to drink another coffee and wait for the command to appear.

Five minutes passed before they heard voices out in the hall. A conversation was being conducted in low, urgent tones.

Tiree guessed it wasn't the taxi driver before curiosity prompted Eloise to go to the door and peek her head out into the hall. She returned to the table, looking a little puzzled.

'It's Uncle Bob. I wonder what he wants... Oh, God, I hope Dad hasn't asked him here to have a talk with me. That would be just so embarrassing.' The girl rolled her eyes at the prospect.

Tiree felt her heart drop like a stone. 'Is Uncle Bob—Dr Chivers?'

'You know him?'

'He was the doctor I saw at the hospital.'

Eloise looked slightly askance at her. 'Were you in there long?'

'No, just overnight,' Tiree dismissed.

'Oh, right.' Eloise made a sound of relief. 'For a moment I thought you might be…well, one of his headcases.'

'Headcases?' Tiree echoed.

Eloise blushed a little, taking it as disapproval. 'Sorry, I shouldn't use that word.'

'You mean mentally ill?' Tiree's question drew a nod of assent. 'Uncle Bob's a psychiatrist?'

'Sort of,' Eloise confirmed, 'although not exactly.'

Tiree wondered how a person could be a sort of but not exactly a psychiatrist. She did not have the chance, however, to elicit any further explanation as the two men appeared in the kitchen.

'Hi, Eloise,' Uncle Bob greeted with a smile, 'how's school?'

'Psychologically damaging,' Eloise responded in deadpan fashion.

It drew a frown from her father even as Bob Chivers laughed aloud.

'Fairly normal, then,' he judged, his eyes sliding to acknowledge Tiree with a slight smile.

'Eloise,' Sinclair distracted his daughter, 'I wondered if you could possibly go down to the village and buy some milk. We seem to be running low.'

Eloise looked ready to object, aware it was an excuse to get rid of her, but when he added, as a sweetener, that she could buy herself a couple of magazines, she was suddenly co-operative.

Tiree could have tried to leave with her, but she was reluctant to involve the girl, so she sat tight.

No surprise when Bob sat down beside her, pouring himself a cup of coffee, while Sinclair followed Eloise out of the room to fetch his wallet from upstairs.

Bob began with the words, 'How's your head?'

'Fine, thank you, Doctor,' she replied in a dry manner.

Sinclair's friend allowed himself a slight smile, before reaching to take a sip of coffee.

Tiree waited for him to state the real reason for his visit but he seemed in no hurry.

'I suppose Sinclair called you out,' she prompted.

'Actually, no, I rang him,' Bob Chivers claimed. 'I was concerned about the false stories regarding your stay at the clinic.'

Tiree shrugged. 'I shouldn't worry. Being thought a wacko will probably enhance my career,' she confided drily.

'Yes, Sinc did say you were taking a philosophic view,' Bob smiled again. 'Still, I thought I'd come over, see how you are, have a chat.'

Bail his friend out, Tiree added mentally, as she guessed the purpose of this house call.

'Will here do—' her tone was sweet but laced with irony '—or do you want me lying on a couch?'

Bob was thrown for a moment, and Tiree wondered if she'd misread the situation, then he gave her a sheepish look.

'Am I so transparent?'

'No, but Sinclair is.'

'Always has been,' Bob ran on. 'What you see is what you get with Sinc.'

'Not always.' Tiree would not have guessed that under Sinclair's remote, clinical exterior lay a man capable of strong, sexual passion.

'Yes...' Bob hesitated before saying, 'He can, on occasion, be impulsive.'

'That's one word for it.' Tiree decided to ask point-blank, 'He's told you what happened between us last night?'

'Not in any detail,' Bob was quick to deny. 'I expressed my disquiet on hearing you were staying here, and, after some hedging, Sinclair admitted that things had become more, shall we say, complicated since I last saw him. I thought I might be of some service, *un*complicating them.'

Tiree realised he was acting in Sinclair's interests rather than her own but he was useful as a go-between.

'Well, you can tell Sinclair to relax,' she replied. 'I am *not* a) going to die of a broken heart, b) report him to the Medical Council, or c) give an exclusive. As in Sad Singer Seduced By Sexy Surgeon Love-Rat!'

Tiree grinned at her own tortured alliteration and Bob Chivers's mouth twitched in humour.

He was serious, however, as he declared, 'Sinclair hasn't mentioned any such fears. His prime concern appears to be for you.'

'Big of him.' Tiree didn't hide her resentment at being treated like some basket case. 'Well, I'm fine. Deeply *un*traumatised. Barely moved, in fact.'

Bob got the message, musing, 'Do I detect a slight note of hostility?'

'More a concerto,' Tiree quipped back. 'I mean...ask yourself. Which one of us is crazier? A deviant, at the very least.'

'Sinclair?' Bob smiled quizzically at the very idea.

'Too right,' Tiree warmed to the subject. 'What else would you call him? He can't wait to sleep with me when he thinks I'm a tart. The moment he discovers I'm not, he goes into full retreat. You explain that one?'

'I could,' Bob replied quietly, 'only I think you're quite clever enough to work that one out... Meanwhile, between ourselves, how *do* you feel?'

Tiree tried to shrug the question off but Bob kept looking at her steadily until she was forced to come up with some kind of reply. 'Dislocated.'

'Dislocated,' he echoed, approving the term rather than disputing it.

There was no pressure to explain further. Maybe that's why she did so.

At first she talked of work and her career, but gradually the conversation rippled further back to the past. She told him things without intending to do so. Perhaps it was because he didn't comment or advise, but merely listened, the essence of a good therapist.

'I suppose you're thinking now,' she concluded, 'that I really am messed up, psychologically speaking.'

'Do you feel you are?'

'Sometimes, but I reckon everyone is in some way.'

Bob acknowledged the truth of it with a dry, 'Just as well or I'd be out of a job.'

'Yes, I suppose.' Tiree had all but forgotten that the conversation was more professional than personal. 'Well, feel free to charge me for this session... Or better still, send the bill to Sinclair.'

'I might at that,' Bob smiled at the idea.

But it sparked off some alarm for Tiree. 'You're not going to tell him what I told you, are you?'

'I can't even if I wanted to,' Bob assured her. 'Patient confidentiality... Anyway, it's your story. Best you tell him as the relationship develops.'

'What?' Tiree studied his expression to see if he was joking. 'I don't think you understand. Sinclair and I, we're not having a relationship.'

Bob raised a brow. 'Are you sure?'

Was she sure? What kind of question was that?

'Ask Sinclair.'

'And what if he says otherwise?'

'He won't.' Tiree wondered why his friend was even questioning it. 'Do you honestly see me as Sinclair's type?'

Bob gave it a moment's thought. 'I wouldn't say Sinclair has a type. He's not a great ladies' man, as such. Unlike Rhys. I understand you met him yesterday.'

She nodded. 'Yes, he was sort of chatting me up but I suspect he chats up everyone.'

'As long as they're young and pretty,' Bob confirmed. 'Rhys must have dated half the girls at Med School. Although, between us, I think some were more interested in Sinclair. For all the notice he took, especially after he met Nicole.'

'His wife?' Tiree guessed.

'Ex-wife,' Bob amended.

'How long were they together?' Tiree enquired.

'Four years, on and off,' Bob relayed. 'Just long enough for Nicole to decide being wife to a junior hospital doctor held little glamour.'

'Did she run away with someone else?' Tiree asked, curious.

'A financier, I think it was,' Bob responded. 'Or maybe it was the writer first. I can't remember... Nicole got bored easily.'

Bob, so studiously neutral in his professional capacity,

seemed quite disdainful and Tiree concluded, 'You didn't like her?'

'I didn't like how she treated Sinclair or the children for that matter,' he qualified, 'but it was hard not to like her on a personal level. She *was* quite charming. Stunning, too, of course.'

Of course, Tiree echoed silently—and a shade sourly.

'How did they meet?'

'She was the daughter of one of our professors, Henry Dunn-Willis,' Bob recalled. 'She'd just left her first husband and the Prof introduced her round at one of his soirées. I'd say it was love at first sight for both of them, although Sinclair would probably deny it. At any rate, it was a case of marry in haste, repent at leisure, which is probably why Sinc is so cautious these days.'

Cautious? Recalling last night, it wasn't a word Tiree would have applied. In fact, maybe *desperate* would be closer, if he hadn't had a girlfriend in a while. It would explain why he'd turn to her.

The trouble was it didn't explain why she'd turned to him.

'I wouldn't let his marital history put you off,' Bob added, 'should that be the issue.'

'It isn't,' Tiree refuted. 'It's more a we-don't-even-like-each-other issue.'

Bob smiled at this claim in a way that suggested he didn't believe her. 'Yet he was your first.'

Tiree blushed furiously, with anger as much as embarrassment. 'He actually told you that?'

'I believe *you* did, in a roundabout way,' Bob responded. 'Sinclair was more circumspect. As I recall, his words were: I took advantage of her vulnerable state.'

Had he? Tiree didn't quite remember it being like that. More a case of mutual lust sending mind, body and morals into free-fall.

'Look, it really wasn't like that,' Tiree declared. 'I don't quite know why we ended up doing what we did. It just happened. He doesn't have to go on a guilt trip over it. Best forgotten, I'd say.'

'That simple? What if there are repercussions?'

'Repercussions?'

'A pregnancy.'

'Not likely,' she dismissed, 'but I'd cope. I'm not this poor, pathetic creature that Sinclair makes out.'

'No, I appreciate that.' Bob gave her an appraising look. 'I don't imagine Sinclair considers you such, either. It's more a case that you're outside his experience.'

Tiree accepted that. 'I bet he normally dates female doctors as po-faced as he is.'

Bob struggled to hide his amusement. 'It's the women he meets. It may not be the kind ultimately right for him.'

'Yeah, well,' Tiree retorted, 'I don't think female androids are available as yet.'

This time Bob laughed out loud, but, then perhaps feeling a disloyalty to his old friend, added, 'Sinclair really isn't as cold and unfeeling as he may appear.'

Tiree might have cast doubt on that claim but remembered last night too well. In one respect Sinclair was far from cold! But that was sex and, as Stu used to say, sex was just sex—a physical act quite unconnected with love.

'You don't have to sell him to me, Doc,' Tiree said at length. 'I'm out of here, as soon as I can organise a lift. So if you'd go and tell him I'm cool about it all, I'd be grateful.'

'You're sure that's what you want?' Bob rose from the table.

'Quite sure.' Tiree rose, too. 'But thanks for listening.'

'Any time.' A smile said he meant it.

Tiree took the hand she was offered and they parted on good terms.

With Bob gone, Tiree started to clear the table of breakfast dishes, stacking them in the dishwasher. She was conscious that once again she was playing domestic in the Sinclair household but she preferred keeping busy to thinking too much about last night. She was wiping down surfaces when Sinclair entered.

'You don't have to do that.'

'I might as well until my taxi comes. You have called one?'

'Not yet. I wasn't sure of your destination.'

'Cottage first, then Heathrow.'

'You're planning to fly somewhere?' He frowned at the idea.

'Either that or go plane spotting,' she quipped back.

'Is everything a joke with you?' he said rhetorically, his tone verging on exasperation. 'Where exactly are you going?'

'I haven't decided,' she admitted. 'I'll see what flights are available.'

'You think that's the solution,' he countered, 'running away?'

'It's *a* solution,' she argued, 'and it certainly beats staying around to provide copy for the newspapers. I mean, have you any idea what it's like, people pushing cameras in your face, blinding you with their flashes, bombarding you with idiot questions like: How do you feel? Did you see the bodies? And is it true you and Stu used to be lovers...?' she trailed off, wishing she hadn't picked that particular example.

Sinclair winced inwardly at it. He seemed to remember that he had suggested the same. How wrong could a person be!

'I can imagine.' He tried hard to be sympathetic now but she threw it back in his face.

'No, you can't!' she snapped. 'At least you were allowed to grieve for Kit in private. No one demanded that you should cry to order or talk about your feelings. And no one called you a hard-faced cow because you wouldn't.'

It wasn't intended as an accusation but Sinclair felt it as such. Hadn't he assumed the same from her behaviour at the inquest?

'Were you close to Stuart Maclennan?' he asked quietly.

'I loved Stu, yes.' Tiree didn't care if the statement was misleading.

Sinclair proved that by adding, 'But he didn't love you?'

Tiree could have said there were many kinds of love but it wasn't a subject she particularly wished to discuss with Ewan Sinclair.

She answered with an offhand shrug, then tried to walk out on the conversation. He stepped in her way and she recoiled rather sharply.

Sinclair's dark brows drew together as he noted this reaction. 'You're not scared of me, are you?'

'Of course not.' She was scared of herself and the churned-up emotions whenever he came too close and held her eyes too long as he was now doing.

'I didn't mean to hurt you last night.' He was obviously still troubled by it.

But Tiree shied away from any more heavy conversations, retorting, 'Don't worry, I've had counselling.'

'Another joke?' he grimaced. 'I suppose I deserve it... If it's any consolation, Bob thinks you're a strong, resilient character whereas I need my head examined.'

'He said that?' Tiree was surprised by the admission.

'Speaking as a friend rather than a psychiatrist, of course,' he qualified with a slight smile.

'You were at Med School together.'

'Yes... What else did he say?'

'Not much,' Tiree claimed, but curiosity prompted her to add, 'Just that's where you met your wife, and that she was both charming and beautiful.'

He raised a brow at this, but went on to confirm, 'Extremely so, yes.'

Tiree felt a little sore. She'd half-expected him to deny it. After all, they couldn't have parted on great terms. She was left wondering if Sinclair had stayed in love with her, regardless.

'How long were you married?'

'Four years, on and off. The first, fairly happy. The next two, not so. The last as miserable as sin.'

'Right.' Nothing like telling it how it is, Tiree thought, his frankness taking her aback. 'What went wrong?'

'What didn't,' he replied with a shrug. 'She liked to party, I needed to study. She wanted London, she got the Home Counties. I earned too little, she spent more. I wasn't much fun, others were... Ultimately she ran off with someone else, but I imagine you know that.'

Tiree nodded. Bob had told her. The surprise was Sinclair's honesty. She sensed it was costing him pride to admit failure and he was hardly the confessional type.

'I just felt you should hear it firsthand,' he stated at her quizzical expression. 'I have had a few relationships since. Nothing long-term, nor am I particularly looking for such, but I'm not what could be called a womaniser, either.'

'I see,' murmured Tiree, although she didn't at all. 'Why are you telling me this?'

'It's important you know, should you and I decide to do something about this...*thing* between us.' Tiree did a double take, but, no, he was completely straight-faced and absolutely serious.

Her first instinct was to laugh, a nervous reaction that she fortunately suppressed. Her second was to run but he had her pinned to the spot with those compelling blue eyes, so she was left sorting out what to say from a list of options.

She was too young. He was too old. She was a rock singer, he a hospital consultant. He spoke posh, she didn't. They weren't even sure they liked each other as people. And, last but not least, the idea bloody terrified her.

He grew impatient at her silence and muttered, 'You may comment if you wish.'

Tiree was induced to be blunt. 'I think you and me—we'd be an absolute disaster!'

He reacted with the barest flicker of emotion, a tightening of that square, handsome jaw, then he responded, 'I suspect you're right.'

No persuasion. No argument. Tiree felt perversely cheated. Shouldn't he at least be trying to talk her round?

When he spoke next, it was to say, 'I'll drive you home.'

'No, it's all right,' she countered, 'I'll get a taxi.'

'You may have a long wait on a Saturday morning,' he pointed out, 'and I've already arranged to drop Eloise off at a friend's house while I take you.'

He sounded bored, as if she was now a problem, one of which he wanted rid a.s.a.p. So much for 'this thing between us'!

He assumed it was a done deal, as he turned to hold the door open for her.

Resigned, Tiree walked out into the hall and he called to Eloise. He called several times but received no response.

'She must be playing her music,' he muttered and took the stairs two at a time.

Tiree waited in the hall. She noticed a couple of cartons of milk on the hat stand. Eloise must have dumped them there on her return.

After some moments, Sinclair came back down, alone. Grim-faced, he announced, 'She's gone…run away, maybe.'

'What?' Tiree was slow to take it in.

'I found this on her bed.' He handed her a newspaper.

It was a national daily. Tiree's eyes were drawn to a two-inch column headed by her name, skipped through a rehash of the same story as last night, then turned to a continuation on page nine, featuring another photograph taken of their flight from the private hospital. This one also included Sinclair in profile, recognisable only if you already knew it was him.

'She must have caught the headline,' he mused aloud, 'and bought it… As I remember, she was a little strange when she returned.'

'Strange how?' Tiree wanted to help.

'I was saying goodbye to Bob in the forecourt,' he recounted, 'and she just ignored us when she passed by. I was going to have a word with her about her rudeness.'

He shook his head, perhaps at his own lack of sensitivity, while Tiree asked, 'Are you sure she's gone? She couldn't be in the garden somewhere, maybe?'

'It's possible.' He was already walking towards the back of the house.

Tiree didn't follow but went to check all the rooms on the first and second floors. There was no sign of her. It was raining outside so she returned to the girl's bedroom to see if her favourite jacket was on a chair or in the wardrobe. No, it seemed to have gone, too.

She met up with Sinclair in the hall again. From his expression, he'd no luck, either, and was hastily shrugging into a coat.

'I'm sorry,' he apologised distractedly, 'I have to go. You'll call a taxi?'

Tiree shook her head. 'Don't be silly. I'll come with you and help you look… Have you a spare coat?'

'Sure.' He frowned, but didn't argue as he handed her a waterproof jacket from the stand.

One of his, it reached Tiree's knees and might have gone round her twice, but she didn't care. She followed him out to the driveway and the garage at the end, climbing quickly into the passenger seat of his car.

He barely allowed time for the metal gates to open before he drove through them and swiftly down the hill. When he reached the T junction at the bottom, he had to make a choice: towards the pub and shop, or away, in the direction of the road leading to Reading.

He sat for a moment, agonising over the decision, and Tiree felt for him. Like any parent, his imagination was probably way beyond Eloise in a strop going walkabout, and already at the point where the girl was in a car with some malevolent stranger.

'Why don't we split up?' Tiree finally suggested. 'You drive that way for a couple of miles. She can't possibly have gone further. I'll walk into the village and carry on out the other side if I don't see her.'

'Good idea.' He approved, but then cautioned, 'You be careful too, all right?'

'I can handle myself, don't worry.' She levelled him one of her streetwise looks before climbing out of the car and waving him off.

She meant it. She'd survived nights living rough in Glasgow. English country lanes held no great trepidation for her.

Any fear was for Eloise. She was nobody's fool but even sensible girls do silly things when they're angry mad.

At that thought Tiree set off at a good pace, ignoring the twinges from her ankle. She came first to the church, glancing into the graveyard but it was deserted. She strode on to the shop; it was empty, too, apart from a middle-aged lady serving behind the counter. She continued on past a couple of cottages with pretty window boxes and ivy-clad walls, then crossed over as the pavement on that side petered out before a corner.

She was limping a little from her sore ankle when she came out of the bend and onto a straight piece of road. Ahead was a bus shelter and, through its Perspex walls, she caught the flash of a familiar fur-trimmed jacket.

She quelled an instinct to call out and approached with some stealth, anxious not to spook Eloise.

It helped that the girl was scrunched down inside the hood of the jacket and seemingly oblivious to the rest of the world.

'Hi,' Tiree greeted her in casual tones.

Lost in her reverie, Eloise was startled initially but didn't take flight. In fact, Tiree caught a glimmer of relief on her face even if it was quickly replaced by classic teenage moodiness.

Tiree guessed that the girl hadn't wanted to run away. The idea was more to punish her father.

Tiree sat down beside her. 'Waiting for a bus?'

'Yes.'

'So where are you planning on going—back to school?'

Eloise muttered back, 'What do you care?'

Tiree supposed she deserved that. She decided on a frank approach. 'You think we lied to you, right?'

'You *did* lie!' Eloise threw back.

'Okay, we lied,' Tiree conceded. 'We just thought it would be better not to tell you who I was.'

'Why?'

'We didn't want to upset you.'

It was the honest answer but Eloise was unimpressed, giving a snort of disbelief.

'Yeah, right.' Her tone was full of hurt pride. 'I bet you think I'm really thick, not working it out—Ti short for Tiree.'

'Why would you?' Tiree echoed. 'I hardly look like Ti Nemo, do I?'

Eloise's eyes fixed on her face and for a moment they were clouded with doubt. 'You are, though, aren't you?'

Tiree nodded. 'For my sins.'

'What does that mean?' the girl queried.

Tiree shrugged. 'It's just a phrase. In this case, I suppose it means I'm Ti Nemo whether I like it or not.'

'You're rich and famous,' Eloise replied, 'you must like it.'

Tiree could have disputed that, but now didn't seem the time for a lecture on the downside of fame. It was more important to talk Eloise into returning home.

'The point is,' she resumed, 'I preferred being just Tiree to you. Not Ti Nemo... You're right to be mad, though. I shouldn't have deceived you.'

Eloise looked slightly mollified, before she recalled, 'It wasn't just you. Dad didn't say anything, either.'

'I know,' Tiree conceded, 'but you have to see he was trying to protect you. He thought you might find it difficult, meeting someone from Kit's band.'

'But why?' Eloise was perplexed. 'I could have asked you stuff about Kit. He was my brother and I hardly knew him.'

'I'm sorry—' Tiree reached out to squeeze the girl's hand '—we've clearly misjudged the situation. I hope you'll forgive us, Eloise. If not me, then your dad. He really has your best interests at heart.'

'I suppose.' Eloise pulled a slight face. 'Where is he now? At home?'

Tiree shook her head. 'No, he's looking for you, too. We split up but he should be coming along in this direction any moment.'

'Great!' Eloise groaned aloud. 'He's going to be angry, isn't he?'

'He may seem it—' Tiree wasn't about to promise otherwise '—but, believe me, underneath he'll just be relieved to find you're okay. So why don't we start walking back now?'

She held her breath, waiting for Eloise to agree. She wasn't about to use physical force.

Eloise contemplated the alternative, before she shrugged, 'All right.'

They rose together and retraced their steps. They were coming out of the narrow bend, when a familiar car passed. Sinclair spotted them but was going too fast to stop.

Tiree suggested they cross to the other side to await his return. They stood outside the village shop where they would be easily visible.

'Did Dad look mad to you?' an anxious Eloise asked as the minutes ticked on.

'Hard to say.' Tiree thought Sinclair always looked fairly grim. 'But don't worry—let me do the talking.'

'Okay.' Eloise wasn't about to argue with that and linked her arm with Tiree's.

They were trading smiles just as Sinclair appeared alongside them. He had to fight an impulse to leap out of the car and start shouting. It seemed that, while he'd been in a state of high anxiety, the girls had been enjoying each other's company.

Tiree saw trouble brewing on Sinclair's face and mouthed the word, 'Don't!' as she slipped into the front passenger seat.

He took the hint and remained tight-lipped, but it was not encouraging.

Tiree ploughed on, regardless.

'Eloise went for a walk to clear her head,' she bent the truth slightly. 'She was a bit upset that we'd deceived her, but I've told her why we did so and how sorry we are.'

'I see.' Sinclair was still recovering from the scare Eloise had given him but followed Tiree's lead as he forced out, 'That's good.'

'And Eloise is sorry that she didn't tell you where she was going,' Tiree added. 'Right, Eloise?'

'Right,' Eloise echoed obediently but with an equal dearth of sincerity.

Then a silence descended as they drove up the lane and through the gates, leaving Tiree in no doubt that stiff-necked pride was an inherited characteristic.

'So we're cool again, yes?' Tiree said, catching Eloise's eye in the rear-view mirror.

'Cool, yeah,' the girl echoed at this prompting.

Tiree stared at Sinclair next, willing him to play his part. There was an ominous pause as if he might start reading the Riot Act instead.

Then his lips quirked slightly before he announced, 'Positively chilly.'

'Funny, Dad.' Eloise rolled her eyes at this poor joke but at least the two exchanged smiles.

Once inside, however, Sinclair reverted to a more serious

demeanour, excusing himself and Eloise for a private conversation in the study.

Eloise shot Tiree an anxious look before disappearing into the room. Sinclair shot her a look, too, warning her not to interfere. Then the door closed behind them.

Tiree could do little else but trail off to the kitchen and brew a fresh pot of coffee. That occupied five minutes and worrying another five before Eloise came to find her.

Tiree blinked at the smiling girl. 'Are you all right?'

'I'll say,' Eloise assured. 'Dad really *was* cool. He just gave me a hug and made me promise not to run away again. And guess what? In return, he won't send me back to school until after half-term.'

It seemed that Sinclair could compromise about some things. Maybe he wasn't quite as unreasonable as he'd first appeared.

'Also, he says you can stay,' Eloise ran on, 'if you like... Please say you will. We can do things together.'

'I...' Tiree was thrown off balance.

Eloise was obviously desperate for her to agree. Tiree didn't flatter herself. The girl was in need of company. The surprise was Sinclair supported the idea. Or had he just found it too difficult to say no?

Tiree was having trouble herself. She took the coward's way out and said, 'I'll have to discuss it with your father first.'

'Great.' Eloise assumed it was a *fait accompli*. 'He's still in his study, I think.'

'I'll go and see him.' Tiree managed to keep any anger out of her voice, reserving it for Sinclair as she went to track him down.

She knocked on the study door and he called, 'Come.'

He was sitting at his desk, possibly waiting for her arrival. Tiree closed the door firmly behind her before she demanded, 'Did you tell Eloise that I can stay?'

'She asked,' he replied, 'and I said that it was fine by me if you wanted to... Should I assume you don't?' he added at her seething expression.

'You know perfectly well I intended to go abroad.'

'To escape the Press attention?'

'Yes.'

'You've managed that here for the last couple of days,' he countered.

'Yes, but for how long?' Tiree didn't trust that the Press wouldn't track her down through the hospital. 'You don't want them camping on your doorstep, do you?'

'No, but I'll live with it if it happens,' he said resignedly. 'I just think it would be better if you remained here.'

'Better for whom?' Tiree's tone became cynical. 'This wouldn't have anything to do with your needing a babysitter for Eloise, would it?'

'Not especially,' he denied. 'I can draft in my housekeeper to look after Eloise if necessary, although you would clearly be her preference.'

'And yours?' she challenged in disbelief.

He took a moment to reply. 'I think you'd be more fun than Mrs Enderby and would cope better with Eloise's moods.'

Tiree supposed it was an endorsement of sorts but she was still suspicious. 'What about you and I?'

'You and I?' His eyes raised to hers but there was a cool indifference in his gaze. 'I accept what you said earlier—that any relationship between us would be disastrous. I would not intend to pursue such. You have my word.'

His tone was formal and Tiree didn't doubt he meant it. His passing desire for her had obviously passed. Was the effect of her charms so ephemeral or did she just not compare with the first Mrs Sinclair?

The last question lingered and, following in its wake, an unfamiliar emotion. She tried to deny it. She couldn't be jealous of a dead woman. Too absurd! But that's what it felt like.

'So, will you stay?' he added at her growing silence.

Tiree had intended to refuse when she'd entered the room. She knew she had. She could still think of all the reasons why, too.

Yet the words, 'Yes, okay,' came out of her mouth and she sensed they'd be life changing.

CHAPTER TEN

TIREE meant to stay a short while, enough to satisfy Eloise's need for company and to allow the Press interest in her to die down, but the days turned into one week, then two.

It was no hardship spending time with Eloise. They went to the cinema together and ten-pin bowling and another shopping expedition, but were just as happy hanging round the house, listening to music and painting each other's nails. It was like having a little sister.

Tiree had imagined the awkward thing would be living in the same house as Sinclair, but it proved otherwise. Perhaps it was Eloise's presence that forced them to make an effort. Or maybe this was the real Sinclair, more easy-going than he'd first appeared, witty and intelligent company when he chose. He kept his promise, too, and didn't try to repeat their brief encounter in his study.

For her part, Tiree almost relaxed into her role as guest cum au pair. She continued to do some of the cooking, having first sought Mrs Enderby's approval. The part-time housekeeper turned out to be a sweet lady in her sixties who worked more out of devotion than need. Tiree took to her immediately, despite Celia Enderby's on-going litany of praise for Mr Sinclair as brilliant surgeon, excellent father and all-round wonderful human being.

Possibly the housekeeper had never witnessed the other side of Ewan Sinclair. Unlikely that he'd tried to seduce Mrs Enderby, although he did show her a courtesy that made the older woman more fluttery when he was around. Wisely, Tiree kept any negative comments to herself.

It would have been hard to voice them, anyway, when she'd allowed him to take temporary charge of her life. He'd given her money for clothes so she didn't have to go back to the cottage and he'd telephoned the police to put a stop to the newspaper speculation that she'd jumped off Beachy Head.

He'd also advised her to contact the band lawyer about her contractual obligations. Tiree, who'd never had much interest in the money side of things, wouldn't have done this without prompting, but was duly relieved to discover that she was now a free agent as far as the record company was concerned.

Les Gray, her manager, was a different matter. The lawyer had given him Sinclair's telephone number and he'd taken to harassing her on an almost daily basis. He wanted his pound of flesh and was insisting she do the arranged tour with a re-formed band. The idea was abhorrent to Tiree, but she felt unable to discuss the matter with Sinclair.

He did not encourage her to confide. If he happened to answer the phone to Les, he handed the receiver over without a word and remained tight-lipped for the rest of the evening.

Tiree could have cried on the Friday—two weeks from the date of her arrival—when the special meal she'd served in the dining room, was interrupted by the ringing of the telephone from out in the hallway.

Eloise got up to answer it and was back immediately to confirm her fears. Tiree excused herself politely, but was still awarded a black look from Sinclair.

'I told you not to call me at this time,' she informed Les, not wasting any greeting on him.

'Why? Does *Sinclair* not like it?' Les gave a mocking twist to the name.

Fortunately that's all Les knew, and Tiree hoped to keep it that way. 'What do you want, Les?'

'You know what I want, Ti,' Les rejoined, 'an answer.'

'You've had that,' Tiree snapped.

'One I can accept,' Les qualified. 'I mean, if I have to cancel this tour, it's going to cost me a packet, which, in turn, is going to cost you a packet.'

'I've told you,' Tiree was tired of this threat, 'I don't care. Go ahead and sue me.'

'Don't think I won't,' he muttered.

'Then while you're at it, Les,' she suggested scornfully,

'why don't you sue Kit and Stu as well for going dead on you?'

She didn't wait for a response but slammed down the phone, and had to stand for a minute or two, composing herself, before she re-entered the dining room.

Both heads turned towards her. Neither smiled. Had they heard her shouting?

She sat down and attempted another mouthful or two of her meal, but the food was now as cold as the atmosphere in the room.

'I'll clear.' She made to rise.

'No, Eloise will do it.' Sinclair gave his daughter a look that didn't invite argument.

'Sure.' Eloise gathered up as much crockery and cutlery as she could carry. 'Will I bring dessert?'

'Not for me,' her father dismissed.

Tiree shook her head, refusing too.

'Coffee?' Eloise added.

Her father reacted with surprise. 'Can you make it?'

'I am twelve, Dad,' Eloise reminded with an expressive sigh.

'Sorry,' her father grimaced in apology. 'Then, yes, please.'

'Please,' Tiree echoed when Eloise glanced her way.

'*Can* she make it?' Sinclair directed at Tiree as soon as Eloise left. 'I don't want her burning herself.'

'She won't,' Tiree assured. 'She's made it several times using the cafetière.'

'Another thing you've taught her.' Sinclair's tone wasn't altogether fond. In fact, it was definitely sarcastic as he wondered aloud, 'What *will* we do without you?'

Tiree didn't know what to say so ignored it.

But Sinclair was no longer prepared to skirt round the issue of her leaving. 'When are you planning to go?'

His manner was so chilly, Tiree found herself retorting, 'Tomorrow, if you like.'

She regretted it instantly. She didn't want to go at all.

'I don't *like*,' he ground back, 'but I prefer to have some forewarning before you disappear on your World Tour.'

Tiree was taken aback. She hadn't mentioned the tour to him.

'Who told you about it?' she asked slowly.

'Not you, anyway,' he replied, his voice curt.

'Les?' It drew a nod. 'When?'

'Three evenings ago when you went for a walk with Eloise,' he informed her. 'He imagined I knew about this tour, of course. In fact, he accused me of standing in your way of going.'

Tiree gave him an apologetic look. Les had told her none of this. 'What did you say to him?'

'Nothing,' he clipped out. 'I find speaking from a position of ignorance isn't advisable.'

'I'm sorry I put you in an awkward position.' Tiree's contrition was genuine. 'I didn't tell you about the tour because I'm not planning on going.'

'Why not?' His manner softened slightly.

'I don't want to sing with a new line-up.' She shook her head. 'It was Stu's band, not mine. I was only in it by default.'

'What do you mean?' Sinclair frowned.

'I filled in for their original female singer once,' Tiree recounted. 'Unfortunately she took offence and walked out altogether. Stu talked me into doing another gig, then another, until it came down to a choice between college or the band.'

'College?' Hadn't she told him she had no qualifications? 'What were you studying?'

'The violin,' she reminded him, 'at Glasgow Royal Academy.'

Sinclair still wasn't sure whether to believe her. She seemed to have lived a very full life for twenty-three.

'Perhaps you could play for me some time,' he suggested.

Nobody's fool, Tiree responded, 'As a test, you mean?'

Sinclair didn't bother denying it, his lips quirking a little as he asked, 'Would you pass?'

'I can play,' she claimed, feeling no need to prove herself.

'In that case, I would enjoy hearing you,' declared Sinclair with some sincerity.

'You might be disappointed,' Tiree felt obliged to warn.

'Even at my best, I'd have probably ended up playing second fiddle in a regional orchestra.'

'Would you have been happier, though?' Sinclair mused aloud.

'Who knows.' Tiree had avoided contemplating what-ifs from an early age. 'A great deal poorer, that's for certain.'

'And money's important?' he concluded.

Tiree assumed he was looking down his long patrician nose and batted back, 'To those of us not born into it, yes.'

'I didn't intend to be patronising,' he appeased. 'I just meant it has to be a major consideration. This tour is likely to be extremely lucrative in light of your current success.'

Tiree was confused. Why was he, of all people, encouraging her to cash in like this?

'That's only on the back of the accident,' she stated bluntly. 'I'd be trading on Stu's death...and Kit's. You can't want that?'

'What I want is scarcely relevant,' he dismissed, although his eyes shadowed at mention of his stepson.

Of late, it had become a taboo subject between them. Not with Eloise. She was desperate to hear about Kit's life and Tiree offered her carefully edited highlights of his time with the band. Sinclair, however, had asked no more searching questions of her; perhaps he no longer wished to know the answers.

'I am simply stating,' he continued in a more formal tone, 'that this could be a very big opportunity you're passing up.'

It probably was but it gave Tiree no grief to do so. She already had money. Not a fortune, but enough. And without Stu and Kit, touring America wasn't an experience she was inclined to repeat.

What really bothered her was Sinclair's attitude. It felt as if he was pushing her to go.

'Look,' she replied heavily, 'if you're desperate to see the back of me, then say so. You don't have to send me on a world tour to get rid of me.'

She made to leave, ostentatiously throwing down her napkin and pushing back her chair to rise.

He rose with her and, when she would have walked away,

he prevented her. Strong fingers curled round her upper arm, and they stood shoulder to shoulder and her heart began to race, simply at his touch.

It made her mad enough to hiss, 'Let me go.'

'Come on, Ti—' his tone was gentle in comparison '—I don't want to fight. I don't want you to go, either. You must know that.'

'Then why are you trying to talk me into this tour?' she choked out.

'Because I feel I should,' he replied, holding her gaze. 'Because I'm afraid you'll regret it, if you don't. But it really has nothing to do with my inclinations.'

Tiree believed him. She could scarcely do otherwise, as he looked at her in a way which made it clear that, for him, the 'thing' between them hadn't died.

And for her? Had she been waiting for this moment, longing for him to reach out a hand to touch her cheek and gently tilt her head upwards? Or was it dread that made her heart beat so hard?

She had little time to find the answers before they were kissing and she ceased to care after that. She surrendered to the feeling of total helplessness as his lips moved over hers, at first soft and persuasive, then urgent and demanding. She let him invade, moaning as he did so. She tasted the red wine on his breath, smelt the tang of his aftershave, twined her arms round his neck. She held him to her, craving the hardness of his body against hers, willing to give herself up to him if only he asked.

That's how they were, locked into each other's arms, when Eloise walked in. She hadn't knocked. Why should she? It was her house. *Her father* was kissing Ti of all people.

The girl stood stock still for a moment, tray in hand, staring from one adult face to the other, before deciding retreat was the best option.

'*Sorry*,' she muttered with an almost amused emphasis as she backed out of the room.

Sanity returned, Tiree sprang apart from Sinclair. Too late, of course. She stared at the closing door, her uppermost feeling concern for Eloise.

'You have to go after her,' she urged him, 'and say something.'

'What exactly?' he returned, pushing a hand through his dishevelled hair.

'I don't know.' She'd never been in this situation before. 'Say we had too much to drink.'

He looked askance at her. 'I hadn't.'

'That's not the point.' Was he being deliberately obtuse? 'You mustn't allow her to get the wrong idea.'

'And that idea would be...?' He gazed at her, one eyebrow raised, waiting for enlightenment.

Tiree took a deep breath and counted to ten. Now she remembered why a relationship between them would be impossible. It was just a pity she hadn't remembered a few moments earlier and saved herself this embarrassment.

'Look, she's your daughter. Say what you like. I'm going to pack.'

'Pack? You can't leave over this.'

'I'd be going home on Sunday, anyway, when Eloise returns to school. I just think it would be easier if I left now.'

'Easier for whom?'

'Everyone.'

Tiree doubted Eloise was going to react well to the kiss. What Sinclair felt was anyone's guess. As for herself, the heart hammering against her ribs warned her of how fragile it was.

'Maybe easier for you, Ti—' he gazed at her hard '—but not for me... Do you want me to apologise for kissing you?'

Tiree shook her head. No, too absurd when they both knew she'd enjoyed it.

'You should go and speak to Eloise,' she repeated.

'If you promise not to pull any disappearing acts?' he countered.

'Yes, all right.' She felt too drained for a moonlight flit, anyway. 'I'm going up to my room.'

Satisfied, Sinclair nodded, then they stood for a moment longer, just looking at each other.

His expression was a little quizzical, as if he was wondering why he was attracted to her. She certainly didn't compare with the tall, elegant blonde his wife had been.

The thought made her tear her eyes away from his and head for the door.

He followed, falling in step behind her on the stairs. 'I imagine she'll be in her bedroom.'

'That's usually where she goes.' Tiree left the words 'when she's upset' unspoken.

Halfway up, they heard the thump of rock music and, at the landing, Tiree recognised the track. She should do. She was singing on it.

The surprise was Sinclair doing so, too.

'You really can sing,' he said as if there was some dispute about it.

Tiree was tempted to say, I know, but he might mistake it for egotism rather than flippancy.

She settled on a polite, 'Thanks.'

'Wish me luck, then,' Sinclair added as they paused outside Eloise's door.

He didn't sound particularly anxious but Tiree was. She didn't want father and daughter to fall out over the situation.

'Look,' she offered, 'if it helps, tell her I threw myself at you. It might go down better.'

'And she'll believe that?' He arched a brow.

'She might.' Tiree remembered the Isabella from Spain incident.

'Ti Nemo,' Sinclair replied, 'making passes at her boring, old father? I really don't think so, do you?'

Perhaps Eloise might regard things that way, but Tiree presumed he didn't. Rather the opposite: she wasn't good enough for the mature, renowned surgeon.

In the end, it hardly mattered. They were a huge mismatch in anyone's eyes.

'Thanks all the same,' Sinclair threw after her, as she climbed the second flight of stairs to her bedroom.

'*De Nada*,' she called back, about the only Spanish she knew.

It's nothing.

Singularly appropriate. Summed up the whole affair, Tiree decided later when she lay in bed, sleepless.

Just a kiss. An admittedly passionate, unarguably pleasurable kiss but of no great significance. Certainly not reason enough to imagine herself in love. Or encourage the idea of him loving her. Or even believe the possibility.

Nothing, so why keep thinking about it? Lie in the dark and wonder if he would ever kiss her again? Fall asleep and dream of it and more?

Tiree had never been a lovesick teenager but she woke up feeling like one. Six hours slumber and she was still obsessing.

'It was just a kiss!' she told her reflection in the mirror.

That definitely helped. Not the words, but seeing herself, puffy-eyed and crusty with sleep. Hardly the object of any man's fantasies, far less Ewan Sinclair who'd spent four years waking up next to blonde, flawless perfection.

Tiree had seen the photographs. None on display, of course. Sinclair wasn't a masochist. But she was, dwelling on every beautiful feature of the woman in Eloise's baby pictures. No need, either. She'd already been told Nicole Sinclair had been knockout, drop-dead gorgeous, without seeking confirmation.

Tiree imagined Sinclair still had photographs in a drawer somewhere. Perhaps he took them out when he wanted to remind himself what he had lost or to ask himself why he was bothering with lesser mortals like Tiree.

Tiree caught up with her train of thought and stopped it dead on its tracks. Jealousy really was a demeaning emotion. She pulled a last face in the mirror and went to shower.

She arrived late for breakfast, but it was Saturday and both Sinclairs were still at the table.

'Good morning,' Sinclair greeted her in a pleasant tone.

Eloise said nothing but she glanced up and awarded her a wide grin.

What *had* Sinclair told her about last night?

She drew up a chair and poured cereal. Eloise continued to smile as if something was amusing her.

'We were just discussing the barbecue,' Sinclair directed at Tiree.

'Barbecue?' she echoed.

'At Bob's house,' he reminded. 'This afternoon... I did mention it to you.'

Once. More than a week ago. In passing. She'd assumed she'd be gone before the event and consequently let it slip from her mind.

'You are coming, aren't you?' Eloise chimed in. 'It won't be much fun if it's just Dad.'

'Thank you,' her dad commented drily.

The two pulled faces at each other, then turned their attention back to Tiree.

'I don't know.' Tiree felt it would be awkward. What was she going as? A friend of the family or the au pair?

Eloise misunderstood, asking, 'Are you worried you'll be recognised?'

Tiree shook her head. She'd already been out in public since the newspaper articles and drawn no notice.

'No, that isn't a problem.' She wondered how best to phrase an excuse.

But Sinclair cut in, 'That's agreed, then. I'll go phone Bob and confirm.'

He scraped back his chair and departed before Tiree had a chance to refuse.

Eloise, however, registered her lack of enthusiasm, asking, 'You do want to go, don't you?'

'Yes, of course.' Tiree had no wish to make a fuss. 'I just thought that as it's your last day before you go back to school, you might prefer to have your dad to yourself.'

'Not especially. In fact, you have my permission to share him if you like.' The girl gave her a slightly knowing smile.

Tiree could have ignored it, but she wanted to set the record straight.

'Eloise, about last night...' she paused to select her words carefully.

Eloise helped her out, 'You and my dad kissing, you mean?'

Tiree wondered if she was the only one to feel any embarrassment over the subject. Eloise certainly showed none. Perhaps she was used to women throwing themselves at Sinclair, witness Isabella from Spain.

'Don't worry,' the girl added, 'Dad's explained it all and I'm okay with it.'

'Right.' Tiree supposed that was good, but her curiosity was roused. 'If you don't mind my asking, what *did* your father tell you?'

'You know Dad. He ummed and aahed a lot before he got to the point,' Eloise confided, 'which was basically he fancies you rotten but I wasn't to take the whole thing too seriously on account of you being much younger and a famous pop star.'

Tiree's immediate reaction was disbelief. 'He said he fancied me rotten?'

'Maybe not those words, exactly,' Eloise admitted, 'but that's what he meant.'

Tiree doubted it. The not taking too seriously, however, sounded like something Sinclair might have said.

'And you must fancy him, too,' Eloise concluded, 'otherwise you wouldn't let him kiss you, would you?'

At this inescapable logic, Tiree conceded, 'Your father is an attractive man.'

'That's a yes, you do fancy him, then?' Eloise smiled broadly.

'I-I…' Tiree didn't know how to answer that one. 'I don't want you to make too much of this, Eloise. You understand?'

'Sure,' Eloise nodded. 'I mustn't go out and buy the bridesmaid dress just yet, right?'

Tiree was taken aback for a moment, then laughed. Maybe Eloise had the right idea. Treat the whole thing as a joke.

'Actually,' she threw back, 'I've already designed it. Sugarplum pink. Bell sleeves. Elasticated bodice. You'll look like a little princess.'

'Ugh!' Eloise put a finger to her mouth and made sick noises.

'You have been warned!' advised Tiree before she noticed Sinclair had re-appeared.

'Warned about what?' He'd only caught the tail-end of the conversation, thank God.

Tiree glanced in alarm at Eloise. What if she told him they'd been discussing bridesmaid dresses?

Eloise's eyes twinkled, contemplating mischief, but mercifully she replied, 'Girl talk, Dad!'

'In that case, I'll mind my own business,' he said equably. 'Has anyone seen my laptop?'

They both shook their heads but Eloise volunteered to go and look in his car.

Sinclair remained. He caught Tiree's eye briefly, before she looked away.

Tiree studied the tabletop. It was ridiculous. Her heart was knocking against her ribs. Was this going to happen every time they were alone? It was tantamount to having an illness.

'I spoke to Eloise about last night,' he volunteered, laughing slightly. 'She thinks it's cool.'

And he, it was apparent, thought it amusing. Well, why not? The two of them were a joke together. Pity Tiree's sense of humour had deserted her.

'You and I,' he added at her silence, 'kissing.'

'I understood,' Tiree snapped before he felt a need to do drawings. 'So we can forget it, right?'

'If that's what you prefer.' His voice held the smallest hint of mockery.

It brought Tiree's head up again. Her eyes went to his. Mistake. He smiled, as if he could see right through her.

'Yes, it is,' she claimed, but they were just words.

They both knew that. How could she forget when he had a way of looking at her that made her recall every time he'd kissed her, touched her, left her longing for more?

Tiree hoped she wasn't blushing but she rather thought she was. She was relieved when Eloise returned, announcing her presence first with some noisy throat-clearing in the hall.

By the time afternoon rolled around, Tiree was almost pleased they were going to this barbecue. Other people might take her mind off Ewan Sinclair. Maybe he'd stop watching her, too. It was unnerving.

'Ti,' Eloise came upstairs to fetch her. 'Dad wants to know if you're ready?'

'Be right down.' Tiree scrutinised her outfit in the mirror one last time.

She'd been limited to a choice of three, all casual. It was a hot June day and she'd plumped for cream-coloured Capri trousers and a sleeveless white T-shirt. She was hoping to blend into the background.

'Is this okay?' she asked of Sinclair who was waiting on the doorstep.

Sinclair was surprised by the question. It was the first time she'd consulted him on her appearance and she looked as she always did to him. Young and waif-like yet sexy as hell. He realised, however, her concern was simply whether her outfit was appropriate for the occasion.

'It's fine,' he said at length.

'He means you're drop-dead gorgeous,' Eloise prompted. 'Don't you, Dad?'

Tiree's expression threatened murder but Eloise laughed all the same.

'Well, that goes without saying,' her father replied gallantly, as he held the door open for them.

He himself was dressed in his usual casual wear, chinos and short-sleeved shirt with a buttoned-down collar. Hardly high fashion, but that was all right by Tiree. He was handsome whatever he wore.

It wasn't far to Bob Chivers's house. Just enough distance for her to become extremely nervous. Sinclair had promised her the Chivers would not reveal her identity but what if she was recognised, anyway?

The sun was high and the barbecue party already humming when they arrived. The Sinclairs obviously felt quite at home; Eloise immediately disappearing inside the house to find Bob's teenage daughters, while Sinc led the way round the side of the elegant Edwardian house to a stone terrace and garden below. As they climbed down the steps, they drew more than a few interested glances. Tiree didn't flatter herself, however. She quickly realised the curiosity was down to Sinclair arriving with an unknown lady in tow.

Most of the guests he shared with Bob as friends and colleagues. They clearly operated as a set, relaxed in each other's company even before the wine flowed.

For the first couple of hours, Sinclair stuck religiously by her side. Perhaps he feared what she might say, given free rein, or maybe he knew from experience that his friends would put her through the third degree.

When she was asked what she did for a living, they answered simultaneously. She said au pair, while Sinclair said musician. Quite a discrepancy but fortunately it amused their audience, who concluded she was an aspiring musician currently employed as nanny.

Civilised people. If they were judging Tiree, they certainly didn't let it show, but still she was glad when the introductions were over and she could relax a little.

It was some time before she met their hostess, Jane Chivers, but she took to her immediately. The feeling was mutual as Jane invited her to chat in the kitchen while she prepared more salad and nibbles. Tiree helped with cutting and chopping while conversation ranged between tastes in food, current reading matter and teenage children. Jane had two of the latter and Tiree contributed her own anecdotes about Eloise.

Tiree was careful to avoid mention of Sinclair but that didn't stop Jane eventually asking, 'So is it serious between you and Sinc, then?'

It was so direct Tiree couldn't take offence. Nor did she feel able to deny any involvement, being certain Bob had said something to his wife.

'I wouldn't think so,' she replied, forcing a laugh.

'Why not? Or shouldn't I ask?' Jane pulled a face, acknowledging her nosiness.

Tiree shrugged. 'I'm not his type.'

'Why do you say that?' Jane had seen the way Sinclair looked at her.

'Lots of reasons.' Tiree felt they should be obvious. 'I mean I hardly compare with his ex-wife, for a start.'

'Nicole.' Jane wrinkled her nose. 'In my opinion, not being like her, is a plus.'

'She was very beautiful, though,' Tiree insisted.

'I suppose,' Jane conceded, 'but she behaved terribly badly towards him. You know she left him?'

'Yes, Sinclair told me.'

'Not just once, but twice.'

Tiree hadn't known that. 'He took her back after the first time?'

Jane nodded.

'Well, there you are then.' Tiree took it as confirmation of how much he'd loved his wife.

'More for the sake of Kit than anything, I'm sure,' Jane added quickly.

Tiree frowned. 'He wasn't Kit's father, was he?'

'No, but that didn't stop Nicole dumping Kit with Sinc, when she bolted with her hot-shot City dealer,' Jane relayed. 'Apparently the new man wasn't up for instant fatherhood.'

'Poor Kit.' Tiree realised how it must have affected him. Small wonder he had been so insecure.

'At any rate,' Jane ran on, 'having care of Kit made it very difficult for Sinclair *not* to agree when later Nicole begged for a reconciliation and, very soon afterwards, Eloise was on the way. Otherwise I doubt it would have lasted as long as it did.'

'How old was Eloise when she left for good?'

'About six months. Went off with a writer who lived in the village. Fortunately they moved away, but it was still hard on Sinclair.'

'And the children?'

'She took them with her that time,' Jane revealed, 'but, when Sinc discovered she'd dumped them on her parents, he sued for custody of both. He was awarded Eloise, but his claim for Kit was weaker... The judge granted each of them access to the other child but Nicole severed all contact when she moved abroad. Kit only came back to him when Nicole died and, by then, it was too late for them to really resurrect the father-son relationship. Not Sinclair's fault, of course, but I suspect he blames himself in some roundabout way for Kit's death.'

No, Tiree could have said, *he blames me.* But she couldn't make a statement like that, without explaining herself, and, though she liked this woman, it wasn't a confidence she wished to share.

From her next comment, Jane was also wondering if she'd said too much. 'Perhaps I shouldn't be telling you all this. I just know Sinclair won't admit how it really was. Maybe it's pride or a desire to protect Eloise, but Nicole is pretty much a no-go area.'

Tiree had noticed. 'Don't worry. I won't say anything to him.'

'Thanks.' Jane gave her a warm smile, then returned to safer subjects.

Later they carried out the salad and other extras, and were arranging them on the buffet table in the garden when someone called both their names.

They turned to find Rhys Williams approaching. He must have arrived when they'd been in the kitchen.

His smile was directed at Tiree, even as he said, 'Jane, you're looking lovely as usual.'

'I wish I believed you, Rhys.' Jane let him kiss her cheek, then wryly advised Tiree, 'Watch this one!' before leaving them together.

Chuckling at the comment, Rhys continued smoothly, 'I was hoping you might be here. We didn't really get a chance to say goodbye the other week… Still working for Sinc, I take it?'

'Yes, sort of,' she confirmed.

'So where is he?' Rhys looked round just as Sinclair appeared, bearing down on them. 'Ah, speak of the devil.'

'Rhys.' Sinclair nodded somewhat coldly, before his eyes flicked to Tiree's face, perhaps questioning where she'd been.

'Sinclair,' Rhys acknowledged, 'you didn't say you were going to be here.'

'I'm rather surprised you are,' Sinc countered. 'I didn't think barbecues were your thing.'

'Thought I'd show my face,' Rhys replied, 'and I'm glad I did now.'

His gaze slid to Tiree, flattering in its intent. Tiree didn't take it very seriously, however. In fact, she almost laughed.

Sinc seemed less amused, although he said to the other man, 'So where's your latest? Or hasn't she been allowed out to play today?'

'Very droll,' Rhys pulled a face, telling Tiree, 'Sinclair thinks my taste in women is a shade too young. How old are you?'

'Twenty-three,' she replied.

'Is that too young? I wonder,' Rhys pondered aloud, 'because, if it isn't, I'm currently a free agent.'

'Really,' Tiree remarked coolly. 'I'll be sure and pass that fact on.'

Rhys got the message instantly and laughed. 'I suppose our man here has warned you against me, too. Well, it's all true but I am open to reform, should you be looking for a challenge.'

'The prize would have to be worth the effort,' Tiree bantered back.

'One way to find out?' Rhys invited with a mildly lascivious look.

It was all show, however, as he realised his charm was wasted on Tiree.

Only Sinclair saw things differently. In fact, one more flirtatious remark from Rhys and he'd want to punch his lights out.

So he walked away instead, growling, 'Don't mind me!'

A disconcerted Tiree and Rhys were left staring at his back.

Rhys eventually spoke up. 'Either Sinc's suffering from sense of humour failure or a certain green-eyed monster has taken possession.'

The former Tiree assumed. Sinc must surely know she wasn't attracted to his friend.

'Talk about irony,' Rhys mused.

'Irony?' Tiree didn't see it.

'Just something about his last au pair. No matter!' Rhys decided his loyalty was ultimately to Sinclair. 'Should we find him and try kiss and make up, mm?'

Tiree hoped she wasn't blushing as Rhys hooked his arm in hers to go looking for Sinclair. They spotted him immediately, standing apart from the crowd. He was not alone, however.

Tiree had noticed the woman earlier. They'd once caught each other's eye and the woman had seemed to stare at her rather disdainfully but Tiree had put that down to imagination.

Tall and elegant in a light pink shift dress and high-heeled sandals, she was leaning towards Sinclair with a body language that spoke volumes.

'Oh, dear,' Rhys murmured, 'beaten to it by the lovely Miss Parker Scott. Have you met Stephanie?'

'No.' The name was familiar, though. Wasn't it a Stephanie whom Eloise had discovered creeping round the house in the early hours?

Feasibly Sinclair knew two different Stephanies but Tiree didn't think it likely.

'Haven't missed much,' Rhys continued. 'Beautiful but deadly... As in deadly boring.'

'*He* seems to like her.' Tiree couldn't help the bitterness in her voice.

It drew Rhys's gaze, as he wondered what was really going on between Sinclair and his young au pair.

'She works in his hospital, that's all,' he replied at length. 'I imagine Sinc feels obliged to make the effort.'

Tiree shook her head. She wanted the truth. 'He used to go out with her, didn't he?'

'Now and again,' Rhys admitted.

A shrug suggested the relationship was casual.

Tiree had no reason to doubt it. Sinclair had once warned her that was the only kind he went in for.

She just hadn't expected it would hurt so much, seeing him with another woman, heads together, talking and laughing, as if they still shared some intimate bond. She wanted to scream at the woman that Sinclair was hers, which had to be crazy.

'Are you all right?' Rhys was watching her closely.

She forced a smile. 'Fine. I think I'll go get a drink.'

'Good idea.' Rhys put a hand at her elbow and steered her to the barbecue area where Bob Chivers was dispensing wine, beer and fruit juice.

The two men clearly knew each other well.

'Rhys,' Bob greeted him, 'you've come! What can I say? I feel deeply honoured.'

'Yes, all right.' Rhys pulled a face at this obvious sarcasm.

'Will I shoot you now or wait till later?' Bob continued in the same vein.

'Later will do, I may be begging you to do so by then,' Rhys drawled, scanning the rest of the party and evidently finding it too tame for his liking.

Bob just laughed good-naturedly before directing at Tiree, 'Sinc was looking for you earlier.'

Tiree's rather fixed smile faltered altogether.

'Well, he's otherwise occupied now,' Rhys answered for her and, rather deftly, changed the subject. 'So is there any chance of getting a drink round here?'

'Certainly.' Bob was reminded of his position as host. 'Help yourself to a beer, Rhys… What would you like, Tiree?'

'White wine, please,' she said in a small voice.

She accepted the glass offered and stared at its contents, rather than catch Bob's eye. She took a mouthful of wine, then another, and tried to concentrate on the men's conversation but it was no use. The words 'otherwise occupied' kept going round in her head. When Rhys directed a question at her, she barely registered it far less was able to find an appropriate response.

She excused herself instead and, ignoring Rhys's concerned, 'Tiree?' she broke away.

Intent on finding a quiet place to be alone, she headed for the steps up to the house. Once there, she slipped through a set of slightly ajar French windows and abruptly came to a halt, when she discovered she wasn't the only person seeking privacy.

She could have backed away without being seen, but she must have been feeling masochistic. Why else would she stand there and watch?

Maybe she needed the full wakeup call: Sinclair with another woman in his arms, the woman's hands linked around his neck, her head tilted for a kiss which never arrived, but solely because Sinclair became aware of Tiree's presence.

At least he had the grace to look guilty. Or perhaps just cross at the interruption. He sounded it as she finally went into retreat and he called out her name.

She didn't stop.

A broken heart was painful enough without witnesses.

CHAPTER ELEVEN

SINCLAIR would have followed Tiree out but the other woman was still clinging to him.

'Oh, dear, was that your little au pair?' Stephanie's voice was mocking.

'She isn't my little anything.' He unlocked the arms round his neck and took a step back.

'In that case, why *can't* we get together again?' Stephanie was still reluctant to take no for an answer.

Sinclair held in a sigh of impatience. He'd already extricated himself once from Stephanie, only to have her pursue him here. If they hadn't had any history, he would have been more ruthless.

'As I said—' in the moment before Tiree had appeared '—I don't think it's a good idea. I'm sorry.'

Stephanie pouted prettily but finally got the message. 'Oh, well! It's your loss.'

She recovered her dignity by walking away, heels clicking, head in the air.

A relieved Sinclair watched her go and allowed thirty seconds before he, too, emerged from the house.

He stood on the terrace and scanned the garden below for a familiar head. He imagined it would be simple to spot her. The cropped dark hair made her stand out from so many identikit blondes.

But it was Bob he noticed first, climbing up the steps from the garden.

'Have you seen Tiree?' Sinclair demanded without preamble.

'Yes, I...' Bob hesitated to tell him, '...I'm afraid she's left.'

'Left? How can she have left?'

'Rhys took her, I believe.'

Bob had expected Sinclair to be angry but wasn't quite ready for his growl of, 'That bastard! That absolute bastard!'

'Sinc!' Bob was conscious they were drawing stares from other guests. 'Let's go inside and talk there.'

'I don't want to talk!' Sinclair almost snarled at him.

Bob ignored it, and Sinclair's attempt to shrug off his hand, as he steered him towards the house.

Sinclair could have got free, but it would have meant taking a swing at the wrong friend.

Bob led him to the privacy of his study and, pushing him into an armchair, poured two glasses of whisky.

He put one in Sinclair's hand but Sinclair rejected it, muttering, 'I'm driving.'

'Okay, but you need some time out first. You can't chase after her in this state.'

'*Chase after her*?' Sinclair looked at him as if he were mad. 'You think I'd do that twice in a lifetime? To hell with it! If she wants Rhys, then good luck to her.'

Bob shook his head but the set of Sinclair's face told him he meant every word.

Tiree would have left the barbecue, regardless. Rhys just made it easier and quicker.

She was backing out of the house when she cannoned straight into him.

'Whoa!' An arm came out to steady her.

'Sorry.' She stared at him without recognition for a second.

'Are you all right?' Rhys enquired.

'No.' Tiree was past pretending. 'Can you take me home?'

'Home? You mean Sinc's?'

'No, *my* home.'

Rhys was hesitant. 'And that'll be okay with him?'

'I imagine so!' Tiree snapped. 'Still, you can ask him when he finishes snogging with Stephanie What's-Her-Name.'

'*Sinc*'s doing what?' Rhys echoed at this unlikely scenario.

'Never mind.' Tiree regretted saying it. She felt jealousy must be leaking out of every pore. 'Can I have that lift or not?'

'Sure.' Rhys felt easier now it seemed he was doing Sinc a favour as well. 'My car's at the front.'

'Great.' Tiree let him put a hand at her elbow.

To all appearances, they left as a couple, but, once in the car, Rhys soon realised that her interest in him was limited to his role of chauffeur.

It was about fifteen miles to the cottage and, with Rhys driving, it took almost the same number of minutes. Rhys tried to make conversation but Tiree was too miserable to bother. Temper had sustained her until she left the Chivers' house. Now it was taking every effort of will not to cry.

When they arrived, there was mercifully no sign of reporters. Two weeks had elapsed and her story was now dead news.

Rhys invited himself in for coffee and Tiree somehow held it together while he was there, but the moment he left, it was as if a dam had burst.

It was so long since she'd cried. Years, in fact. But once started, she couldn't seem to stop.

She cried for Stu. She cried for Kit. She cried for herself and the fool she'd been.

For hadn't Stu told her often enough that love was for suckers?

'Do you love the girl?' Bob dared to ask, as Sinclair sat staring into the untouched glass of whisky.

'*Love*?' Sinclair gave him a pitying look. 'Define love, Bob, why don't you?'

Bob considered his answer, before saying, 'It's different things to different people.'

'Where did you read that—on a cheap Valentine card?' Sinclair sneered in reply. 'I'll tell you what love is. It's a fantasy, illusion and delusion, a form of madness brought on mostly by the ache in your groin,' he added with crude eloquence.

Bob raised a brow, but wasn't really shocked. Sinclair was his oldest friend and he'd seen him in this mood before.

'Interesting,' Bob mused in his best psychiatrist's manner. 'Does that lot mean you are or are not sleeping with the girl?'

'The latter,' Sinclair admitted sourly, 'although my sex life is scarcely your business.'

'Why not?'

'Remind me to enquire about yours some time.'

'I *meant*,' Bob stressed, 'why haven't you been sleeping with her? You like her. She likes you. You're living in the same house.'

'Don't you think I wanted to?' Nightimes Sinclair had thought of little else. 'It isn't that simple. Women like Stephanie, you know where you are. You're not their first. You're probably not their fifty-first. But that's fine. You aren't obliged to be something other than you are or offer anything more than you can give… You understand what I'm saying?'

'You can shag and run?'

'No!… Well, yes…I suppose.'

'But with Tiree, it's different,' Bob surmised. 'Because she was a virgin?'

'Partly,' Sinclair conceded, then rounded on him, 'Who told you that?'

Bob remained silent, realising he'd said too much.

'Tiree?' Sinclair guessed for himself. 'So what else did she tell you?'

'Sorry,' Bob pulled a face, 'you know I can't say. Patient confidentiality.'

'Great,' Sinclair grimaced in return, 'so you probably know more about the damn girl than I do?'

Bob spread his hands. He wanted to help but couldn't. 'You need to ask her, Sinc, if you're going to have any kind of relationship. Just be ready for the answers.'

'Is there any point? Chances are she doesn't want a relationship.' Sinclair had no reason to believe she did. 'Why should she? She's a famous rock star, for heaven's sake. I can just see her settling for a middle-aged doctor with a life about as exciting as fly-fishing.'

'Don't tell me!' Bob didn't hide his exasperation. 'Something Nicole once said?'

Sinclair acknowledged the fact with a grudging, 'What if it is?'

'You want my opinion?' Bob ran on.

'No!'

'Well, I'll give it, anyway. You made one mistake in your life—a biggie admittedly—and you've let it colour your judgement ever since.'

'Thank you, Dr Freud,' Sinclair countered sarcastically. 'And is this your professional or personal opinion?'

'An amalgam of both,' Bob told him.

'Does that mean I have to pay for it?' Sinclair enquired drily.

'Naturally,' Bob claimed, deadpan, before forcing them back to the subject, 'The point is, Sinc, that whoever else she is, Tiree is *not* Nicole.'

Sinclair knew that. 'God, would I love her if she were?'

'So you do love her.' Bob allowed himself a smile.

Sinclair pursed his lips and refused to incriminate himself further.

'Then you'll go after her?'

'What do you think?'

Tiree believed it was a reporter at first. Who else would be rude enough to rap like that on the door?

She'd just come out of a shower and was slipping into fresh underwear when it started. A loud, continuous knocking that didn't allow time for anyone to answer.

Not that she intended to. It was just curiosity that sent her to the window, knotting a towelling robe round her as she went.

She froze when she saw who it was. She had not expected him. When he hadn't arrived in the first hour, she'd assumed he was still otherwise occupied.

'Tiree!' He spotted her, his eyes drawn upwards as if by magnet. 'Come on. Open up. We need to talk.'

'Go away!' Tiree mouthed back. She didn't need to talk. What was there to say?

'*Tiree*!' Sinclair rattled the door handle as she made no move to come down. 'I'll break in if I have to.'

Tiree realised his temper was rising but she was more resentful than scared. Why should *he* be mad?

She tried to stare him down and thought she'd won when he

stepped away from the door, but that was only to be sure she could see him, skirting round to the back of the house.

She watched until he disappeared, then the not knowing sent her downstairs. She found him outside the kitchen window. It had been repaired in her absence but here he was, standing with a brick in his hand. Was that what he'd used last time to break and enter?

The staring competition began again, as each waited for the other to back down.

Tiree cracked first, reaching for the telephone receiver on the wall. 'I'm phoning the police.'

'Go ahead,' he called back.

He had to be bluffing. 'Don't think I won't. And how's that going to look in the newspapers, DOCTOR STALKS FEMALE ROCK STAR?'

'You think I care.' He raised the brick to shoulder height. 'You'd better step back. We don't want you to be cut by any flying glass, do we? Rhys mightn't think you so pretty, then.'

Tiree stared at him for another moment, wondering if he really had gone mad. What had Rhys to do with anything? He was the one who'd been cozying up with his ex-girlfriend.

'This is ridiculous!' She broke first and, striding to the back door, shot the bolt and flung it open. 'What do you want, Sinclair?'

'I'll take that as an invitation.' Sinclair ensured he got his foot in the door.

Tiree backed away, as he came inside.

He walked through the kitchen and out into the hall, glancing upstairs, then into her sitting room.

'Rhys has gone?' he finally threw at her.

'Did you see his car out there?' she threw back.

His lips went into a thin, angry line. 'So why aren't you dressed?'

Tiree guessed the two questions were linked, and wanted to pay him back for some of the hurt he'd caused her. Maybe he was here now, acting like a jealous maniac, but two hours earlier he'd been locked in an embrace with someone else.

'Now, why do you imagine that is?' she retorted, striking a

thoughtful pose. 'What could I possibly have been doing before you arrived?'

'For Rhys's sake, you'd better be joking,' he growled back.

Tiree saw she'd hit target from the muscle working at his temple and the way he clenched and unclenched his hands. She chose not to goad him further. Though she was certain all that repressed anger would never translate into violence towards her, Rhys was another matter.

'I had a shower, that's all.' Her tone was bored rather than defensive. 'But since we're trading that kind of information, where's the girlfriend?'

'If you mean Stephanie Parker Scott—'

'Unless that was someone else you were kissing in the house.'

'Actually, I wasn't,' he pointed out.

'No, silly me, I forgot,' she countered. 'I wandered in and spoilt the moment.'

'It wasn't like that.' He spoke with some restraint. 'Steph is an ex-girlfriend, I admit. And, yes, she wanted me to kiss her... But, no, I wasn't planning to.'

He sounded so convincing, Tiree was tempted to believe him, but she shook her head in the end.

'Look, what else can I say? I'm not interested in bloody Stephanie. In fact, I never really was,' he confessed bluntly, 'but I'm a thirty-eight-year-old man who needs company from time to time and she was willing enough to provide it.'

Tiree wondered if she was meant to feel better, having this explained.

'Well, thanks for sharing that,' she rounded on him. 'So what was I, then? Another easy lay, I guess.'

She spat the words at him, not caring if they sounded crude.

The last thing she expected was for him to laugh. He actually laughed.

Then he stared at her in disbelief. '*You—easy*? You think it's been easy, night after night, knowing you're just a flight of stairs away? Wanting you so badly I can't sleep. Too scared to make a move in case I chased you away.'

Tiree stared back at him. There was such raw passion in his voice it almost frightened her.

He closed the gap between them and caught her arm when she might have walked away. 'Do you feel anything for me?'

Overwhelmed, that's how Tiree felt, but she couldn't possibly tell him that. It wasn't what he wanted to hear. Love—the emotional kind, at least—wasn't on this man's agenda.

'No?' He turned to cup her face in his hands. 'Then I'll make you feel it.'

She gazed at him in mute protest, but if Sinclair saw that vulnerable look, he closed his eyes to it.

Tiree should have had the perfect defence. All she had to do was not respond, and that used to come naturally.

But it was different with Sinclair. She was trembling as he placed his lips to her temple, her cheek, the lobe of an ear. She was swaying towards him even before an arm went round her neck to hold her closer. She was raising her head, seeking his mouth with hers, moaning for his kiss and the turmoil it brought.

It had to be enough that she loved.

Enough that he needed her, breathing hard after that first kiss, openly begging, 'Let me.'

No pride left, either, just an urgent, 'Yes.'

Then his hand closed over hers, and she found herself being pulled up the stairs. He wasted no time or words but took the first bedroom. It just happened to be hers.

He was already kissing her, caressing her, pushing aside her robe as they sank back against the bed.

It was still light. Nowhere to hide from his eyes. Her breasts were bare, but it was her face he gazed at when he began to touch her.

Sinclair wanted to see her lips fall open slightly, hear her gasp as he fingered a nipple until it stood proud. He wanted to watch her eyes dilate, her head go back before he bent to put his mouth to her pert flesh and lap at it with his tongue.

He needed to know she was willing, although there could be little doubt of it, as she held his head there, groaning at what his lips and teeth were doing, urging him to tug harder till pleasure could barely be distinguished from pain. When Tiree grasped at his hair, it was only to move his clever mouth to service her other breast, desperate for the same rough, sweet loving.

She gave no resistance as his hands began to roam over her body, exposing more skin for him to touch. She sat up for him as he pushed the towelling robe from her shoulders. She lay down again when he'd removed the garment and left her naked but for a pair of tiny briefs.

He stood by the bed, gazing at her, eyes dark with desire. It made her shiver and he must have thought she was cold, as he unfolded the counterpane at the foot of the bed and drew it over her. Then he started to pull off his own clothing.

He did so without a trace of self-consciousness. He was as lean and muscular as Tiree remembered. He was also patently aroused, and she shied from him a little.

When he lay down beside her, she was facing away. He kissed the back of her neck and reached an arm round her. He cupped her soft flesh, and its fullness swelled against his palm. She turned to offer herself. He put his mouth to her breast once again and she held him to her, the small animal noises hers as he suckled there.

He moved between breasts, teasing with his tongue and teeth, causing her to arch to him to appease this thing that coiled and uncoiled in her belly. He made her wait, made her want the hand that slipped between silk and skin, barely flinch at the gentle parting of her thighs that found her already warm and wet. A finger made her more so, rubbing against the nub of her flesh, slow and strong, drawing gasps of pleasure with each stroke until she groaned in sweet complaint and closed her legs around him.

It was then he straddled her, his face a mask of desire, and, though she wanted him, Tiree tensed as he pushed inside her, long and hard. She cried out a little, more in shock than pain, and braced herself for the next thrust.

None came. He went still, as he had the first time.

She opened her eyes and looked into his. The tenderness there was echoed in his whisper of, 'I don't want to hurt you.'

Tiree couldn't speak, but she put her lips to his, and kissed him in a way that made him forget his scruples.

Sinclair began to move inside her, slowly at first, infinitely slowly, until she knew the pleasure of it and began to raise her body to meet the rhythm of his. Then it became harder to hold back, harder to remember she was a novice as she tilted her hips to the thrust of his, impossible to resist the desire to penetrate her deeper and deeper as she writhed beneath him, wanting to possess her totally even after they came together in a shuddering climax.

He drew her to him, then fell back against the bed. Spent, they lay in each other's arms until their breathing slowed and shadows lengthened across the room. They didn't talk. What words were there left to say?

He stroked her hair and Tiree fell asleep for a little while. She woke to a different kind of touch as he began to make love to her once more. He explored her body with his skilful hands and his clever mouth, and this time drew out the foreplay until, losing any vestige of inhibition, Tiree begged for him to enter her. He raised her hips to his and drove inside her and she moaned aloud as they coupled until they were slick with sweat and love.

Afterwards Tiree lay staring at the ceiling, aware of Sinclair, propped up on an elbow, watching her. She risked a glance towards him. He reached out to trace her features with a lazy finger.

'I suppose you know you're beautiful,' he finally murmured.

'Of course,' she replied, making a joke of it.

It was better than saying what she really thought: that next to his wife she would seem quite *un*beautiful.

'Then let's see, what else can I say?' Sinclair smiled down at her. 'You're clever, irritatingly so at times. Charming and alarming in equal measure. Absolutely delightful in bed… And I think I may be in love with you.'

The last was added in a lower voice, like a guilty secret.

At first Tiree didn't react. She heard him. She just didn't believe him. It sounded so much an afterthought—something he felt obliged to say. It made her angry.

She sat up away from him, hugging the counterpane to her chest. The move took Sinclair by surprise but he realised he'd displeased her. 'You didn't want to hear that, did you?'

She shook her head and, when he reached a hand out to touch her naked back, she edged further away.

'I don't need lies,' she told him, refusing to turn in case he saw the spark of tears in her eyes. She didn't need his pity, either.

She scrambled to the far corner of the bed, grabbed her robe and made for her bathroom before he could stop her. She locked herself in and leaned against the frame. Pathetic, she knew, to behave like this.

What was his sin, after all? It was a thing men did. She knew that from friends. They confessed love in the aftermath of sex. No matter if in the next moment they were dressed and gone.

She braced herself for a knock on the door but none came. She imagined him moving about in the other room, finding his clothes, pulling them on, already elsewhere in his head. Perhaps he was actually grateful to her, making it easy for him to slip away.

But she didn't want him to be grateful. She wanted him to kick the door down, then beg her to listen. She wanted him to say he really did love her, that he couldn't live without her. Anything but this terrible silence between them.

She began to cry and stepped into the shower once again, turning it on to drown the sound. She stood under the cascade of water while the traces of their lovemaking washed down the drain. Yet she didn't regret it. That would be too hypocritical when she knew she would do it all over again, if he asked.

Fifteen minutes passed before she climbed out and wrapped a towel round her. The shower had helped her regain her composure. Not that she probably needed it. With no sound coming from the adjoining room, she presumed he'd left.

She was wrong, however. He hadn't gone. He had dressed but then sat down on a window seat to wait.

Sinclair read her alarmed expression and said in leaden tones, 'Sorry to disappoint, but we need to talk.'

Tiree took it as a rebuke and coloured. She knew she had behaved immaturely by running. Now all she could do was adopt a front.

'What about?' she asked, with a fair semblance of indifference.

His eyes narrowed, as if trying to look beyond it. 'You tell me. I thought we'd just become lovers, but your subsequent behaviour suggests otherwise.'

'I...we...' In the face of his frankness, indifference had rapidly descended into incoherence. 'I...I don't know.'

'Is it the sex,' he continued in the same vein, 'or what I said afterwards that made you take off?'

'I-I-I...' She was actually stammering now. 'I...um... I'd like to dress.'

He pursed his lips at this non-answer, before he noticed she was shivering. 'Go ahead.'

Tiree crossed to her wardrobe and took out jeans and a fresh T-shirt, then retrieved underwear from a drawer. She laid the fresh clothes on the bed but did nothing else until Sinclair realised she was shy about dressing in front of him and turned to stare out of the window.

With any other woman, he would have considered it ridiculous but Tiree wasn't any other woman. Sometimes she even seemed closer to a girl. Confident, full of attitude, irreverent, but barely grown-up in other ways. Street-wise and savvy, yet a virgin until twenty-three. He realised there were things he didn't yet understand.

When he looked round again, she was standing with her arms crossed in a defensive pose.

'Look, if I'm moving too fast for you,' he told her, 'then I'm sorry. I'm just too old for games.'

Tiree's brow creased in bewilderment. Did he really think it was a game to her?

'I don't know what you want of me,' she answered honestly. She'd never been in this situation before.

'In the short-term, I'd like you come back to the house with me—'

And in the long-term? Her eyes asked the question.

But he avoided it with a vague '—we'll take it from there.'

Tiree wanted to believe in happy endings. She would go and live with him and, who knows, if she was careful to do the right thing, she might never have to leave.

But she'd been down that road once before. On approval. Unable to live up to expectations no matter how hard she tried. She'd come a poor second to the baby the Chisolms had wanted.

Maybe she'd come a poor second to Sinclair's ex-wife, too.

'I can't.' She appealed for him to understand. 'I like you, Sinclair. I more than like you. But you know we're not suited—'

'That's just not true,' Sinclair cut in, his tone ragged. 'You suit me, Ti, and half an hour ago, I could have sworn I suited you.'

Tiree coloured at the illusion but didn't deny it. 'I suit you now, okay, but what about later? When you start noticing that I don't quite match up. Perhaps I don't talk posh enough. Or maybe I'm too young? Or not educated enough?' she fired at him. 'What then? Do I get booted out like some unwanted puppy?'

'Ti—' Sinclair heard the anguish in her voice and rose from the window seat to walk towards her.

'Stay there!' She warded him off before he could touch her.

'I'm not going to hurt you—' he promised quietly.

Tiree scoffed in return, 'Yeah, that's what he said, too.'

'Who said, Ti?'

Tiree realised she was sounding irrational and shook her head.

'*Who said*?' Sinclair insisted.

'Tom,' she responded dully, 'my foster-father. He used those words just before he…he… Look, it doesn't matter.'

'Yes, it does.' Sinclair suspected it mattered hugely.

What had Bob said, again? Ask her, and just be ready for the answers.

'Trust me, Ti,' he added quietly.

'He said that, too,' Tiree recalled every bitter detail. 'No need, really. He already had me pinned on the bed by then.'

Sinclair's face constricted as he shared her pain and her contempt. 'The bastard tried to rape you?'

'I'd say so. Only the cavalry came, his ever loving wife.' Sometimes Tiree wondered if she didn't hate Margaret more. 'Took one look and decided *I'd* led *him* on. Forget the fact I was crying and my knickers were ripped and I was fourteen…'

Sinclair could hear the anger in her voice, the sense of betrayal. It had obviously sustained her over the years.

'What happened after that, Ti?'

'Not much. I returned to the children's home, branded a troublemaker, and they went back to being Mr and Mrs Respectable. End of story.'

Only it hadn't been. Sinclair understood that. The childhood assault had coloured her view on life, making it hard to form adult relationships.

'He wasn't prosecuted?'

'I didn't report it.'

Sinclair worked out the reason for himself. 'You didn't expect to be believed.'

'My word against theirs,' Tiree shrugged. 'Stu reckoned it wasn't worth the hassle.'

'You knew Stuart Maclennan then?' Sinclair remarked in surprise.

She nodded. 'He was in the same children's home. Well, winters, anyway. Summers Stu'd go walkabout. That's what he called it, though Glasgow streets and the Australian outback haven't too much in common.'

She relayed this tale in a manner that betrayed her ongoing feelings for Stuart Maclennan. Not her first lover, but perhaps still her first love.

Sinclair said nothing. He didn't trust himself to contain his jealousy.

'Anyway,' she ran on, 'Stu helped me get my revenge. I wouldn't have had the courage on my own, but Stu was fearless. We didn't even have to break in. I still had my key and the Chisolms were too stupid to change the alarm code. We trashed that house so badly it must have cost them a fortune to put right.'

Tiree's admission was deliberate. This was no longer just a trip down memory lane. It was a test.

She watched closely for Sinclair's reaction. It was mild, the slightest raising of his brow.

She still went on, 'I did other things, too, when I was sleeping rough. Stole from shops, begged on street corners, turned a blind eye when Stu earned money in the worst possible way. So you see, I'm not exactly the kind of girl you'd bring home to your mother.'

'I haven't got a mother.' Sinclair closed the gap between them.

'Or introduce to your friends at the Golf Club,' she added, even as she let him take her hand.

'I don't go to the Golf Club—' he laced her fingers with his '—and certain of my friends already like you too much.'

The latter was said with the trace of a smile and the way he was looking at her suggested he didn't care about her past, just their future.

Tiree still didn't trust that it would be that easy. 'What I'm trying to say, Sinc, is that I can't become someone else for you even I wanted to. I've tried that before and it didn't work.'

'God, Ti—' his surprise was genuine '—why would I want to change you? Forget that you're young and beautiful, you're also funny and bright and maddening.'

'Thanks.' Tiree wasn't sure about the maddening part but the rest made her face glow.

'Whereas I'm a thirty-eight-year-old single father, with one failed marriage behind him.'

'Well, I like you, anyway,' Tiree declared, drawing a wry smile from him.

'But it's not exactly the profile you'd seek in a life partner, is it?'

'I don't know.'

Tiree wasn't going to dare look beyond tomorrow with Sinclair.

A wise course, it seemed, as he hastened to say, 'Not that I'm expecting that level of commitment from you—just come home with me for a while. See how it goes. No strings. I won't try to tie you down.'

'Sinclair—' she cut in '—stop getting in a sweat. I'm not hearing wedding bells. I won't be rushing out to book the church.'

'I think we may have our wires crossed,' Sinclair murmured, but decided to leave it there. 'Never mind. Whatever you want, I'm *cool* with it.'

'Don't,' Tiree urged but with a smile.

'Don't what?'

'Use the word cool. I'd prefer you to stay…um…'

'Pompous?' he suggested.

'Dignified,' she amended.

'Dignified?' He pretended to weigh it up. 'Yes, I like it.'

Then he kissed her, chasing away any last doubts about the relationship, and soon they were behaving in a most undignified manner.

Love, Tiree discovered, could be glorious.

CHAPTER TWELVE

TIREE seized the chance of some happiness but lived in the present, loving him more as time went on without trusting that it would last.

Eloise had returned to school after Whitsun and Tiree had simply stayed on. Now Eloise was due home for the summer and Sinclair wanted to tell his daughter the truth while Tiree was set against it.

On the eve of Eloise's homecoming, they had their first really big argument as a couple. He accused her of hypocrisy. She accused him of insensitivity. It escalated into a slanging match. Tiree stomped off to her room to play her violin, loudly and furiously, until Sinclair appeared in a similar passion and proved that making up was almost worth the fight.

Tiree got her way. Eloise was kept in the dark. It was, however, not the easiest of options as they hid their feelings and, like guilty lovers, spent their nights creeping between bedrooms.

Then one morning they slept late and were frantically dressing when Eloise walked in.

She looked from Tiree, dragging on her jeans, to her father, pulling on his socks, reacted with bare surprise, and, before they could utter a word, retreated, grinning.

Sinclair didn't seem in the least put out, either. In fact, he joked, 'Well, you'll have to make an honest man out of me now.'

'Very funny.' Tiree wasn't amused at all. 'What's she going to think?'

'She's going to think,' Sinclair echoed, 'that we're madly in love, which we are. Then she's going to think I wonder how this'll work to my advantage. Perhaps she'll con one of us into buying that new music centre she wants… You're the only one who has a problem with this, Ti.'

'Yes, well, it doesn't seem right.' In some ways, Tiree was the more old-fashioned of the two.

Yet she wouldn't have predicted his response. 'Then make it right—marry me.'

She stared at him, expecting a laugh to follow, a smile at the very least. Nothing. He seemed perfectly serious.

'Because of Eloise?'

'No, because of you and me and the fact we're perfect together.'

'But...but you didn't want any commitment,' she reminded him.

He looked genuinely blank. 'Excuse me, but you were the one who was scared witless by the idea... And from your current expression, I suspect you still are.'

'I...no...I-I...' Tiree found she was actually stammering.

'Just think about it,' Sinclair advised. 'No pressure. No need to run for the hills. Okay, Ti?'

'Okay,' she echoed weakly.

'Play your violin instead,' he suggested, only half-joking.

She grimaced a little, but he ignored it and, placing a quick kiss on her mouth, rose from the bed to go downstairs.

Think about it? he'd suggested as casually as if they'd been talking holidays or a new suite.

Ti could think of nothing else through the long hot day and some fairly pointed remarks from Eloise. She was still thinking about it when Sinclair breezed in from work and behaved as if he'd forgotten the whole conversation.

Even when Eloise disappeared at the coffee stage, with a knowing, 'I'll leave you two alone,' he didn't broach the subject, but sat talking of other things until she felt like screaming.

Finally she blurted out, 'Did you mean it this morning? About us getting married?'

Her tone was scarcely encouraging. In fact, it was aggressive enough to make Sinclair hesitate to form any reply.

'If you've changed your mind—' she added, jumping to conclusions.

'Not in the least,' he cut in. 'I was just giving you time to make up yours.'

'I have.' Tiree swallowed hard. 'But first I have to tell you about Kit.'

A silence followed. She had broken a taboo.

'I don't need to hear this, Ti,' he said at length. 'Nothing you say will make a difference to the way I feel.'

'But I need to tell you,' she added. He had to know the worst.

She started speaking, half-expecting him to interrupt, but he didn't. First she tried to explain what it was like to be in a band, the ups and downs, the sleeping in vans to save on hotels, the gigs in pubs and clubs and student bars, playing to audiences that are only there for the beer. Then one day the hard work pays off and there's even more hard work, a whistle-stop tour, driving from place to place, concert every night, party afterwards, the resultant exhaustion, the temptation to take something just to keep up with the mania around you.

That's how Tiree finally worked round to revealing Kit's drug habit.

She wondered if Sinclair had understood her, at first. He barely reacted even when she told him outright. Kit had been a user of amphetamines and cocaine.

'You knew?' she surmised at length.

'Not as proven fact,' he told her, 'but I had my suspicions when he visited round the Christmas time.'

Tiree realised rather late that Sinclair had been bound to spot the signs. He was a doctor, for heaven's sake. Even if he hadn't been, he was no fool.

'I debated saying something,' his mouth twisted, 'but in the end I decided the risk of alienating him far outweighed the chances of him actually taking my advice. I regret it now, of course. Maybe I could have got through to him.'

Tiree shook her head, denying that his actions would have made any difference. 'It wasn't the drugs that led to his accident. Well, not directly.'

Sinclair waited for her to go on. She was right, after all. He needed to know this.

'He wanted to get clean so, after the final leg of the European tour, I let him come and stay at the cottage,' she resumed. 'I figured it would cut him off from his supplier.'

'Who? Stuart Maclennan?' he challenged.

Tiree gave a slow nod. She didn't really want to betray Stu but, as good as he'd been to her, he'd been bad news for Kit.

'It worked, too. It wasn't easy, but he did it,' Tiree revealed with a measure of pride.

'And then…?' Sinclair prompted.

And then the worst night of her life, every detail burned into her skull, every word recalled for him now…

Kit said, 'Stu phoned,' and her heart dropped along with the shopping bags she'd been carrying.

'He's back from Brazil?' Tiree hoped he wasn't.

Kit's grin said otherwise. 'He's coming down.'

'Here?' Silly question.

Kit finally picked up on her lack of enthusiasm. 'Should I have told him not to?'

'No, of course not.' Tiree would do that for herself the moment she could slip upstairs.

She waited ten minutes, not to make it obvious, then used the phone in her bedroom to ring Stu.

'You can't come down here,' she said, dispensing with any pleasantries.

'And I've missed you, too, Ti dearest,' Stu drawled after the barest of pauses.

'I'm serious,' she insisted.

'So am I. I *have* missed you.' He spoke with apparent sincerity Ti was almost taken in.

Then he ran on, 'Not that I expect the sentiment to be returned. I understand you've had company.'

'Yes.' Ti expected some sarcasm to follow and Stu did not disappoint.

'So is it love?' Stu enquired. 'Or just lust?'

Ti, who'd been debating the same issue for a couple of days refused to comment.

Instead she repeated, 'You can't come down, Stu.'

'And this would be because?' he queried, amused rather than put out.

'Well, if you must know—' she really wasn't sure about telling him this '—Kit's clean and he'd like to stay that way.'

A brief silence ensued before Stu got back in his stride. 'Now there's a coincidence. I'm clean myself.'

'Yeah, I bet,' Ti retorted.

'Scout's honour,' Stu added. 'Nothing stronger than coffee has passed my lips for three weeks.'

She still didn't believe him. 'Stu, this is Ti you're talking to, remember.'

'Okay, okay,' he gave up the pretence, 'how about if I promise not to bring anything with me?'

'No.'

'I'll be good.'

'No, Stu.'

'Please, Mouse,' he lowered his voice, 'I need to talk to someone real.'

Tiree meant to stand firm but Stu had a way of getting round her. She recognised his little-boy-lost routine yet it still worked on her.

'Not one single upper or downer or any of the other chemicals you put in your body, Stu,' she warned as she finally yielded.

'Yeah, sure,' Stu agreed too easily. 'Thanks, Ti... I'll see you soon.'

She was so wound up by the time Stu put in an appearance, it was almost inevitable she relaxed when he proceeded to be all charm and good humour. There was no one funnier than Stu when he chose—the trouble was he also turned on a sixpence.

He must have noticed straightaway that Kit was behaving differently round her but he refrained from making any comment until the meal was over.

Then he suddenly asked, 'So are you two an item or what?'

Tiree gave him a warning look, while colour suffused Kit's cheeks. Neither discouraged Stu.

'Yes? No? Or you're thinking about it?' he offered them multiple choice.

'*Stu*!' This time Tiree's expression threatened murder.

Kit, however, rose to the bait. 'I like Tiree, sure. Is that a problem?'

'For me, no.' Stu smirked. 'I can't speak for Ti, of course.'

'Just shut up, Stu.' She knew this game but, for once, she refused to let Stu do her dirty work for her.

Another day or two and she'd gently discourage Kit. Right at the moment, he was still vulnerable and it would hurt him.

'What did I say?' Stu's eyes widened in innocence.

Ti would have left it there but Kit surprised them both by muttering, 'Anyone would think you're jealous.'

Ti's heart sank, as she watched the last vestige of Stu's good humour go flying out the window.

'Me? Jealous?' he scoffed. 'Like that would be right. In case it's slipped your notice, Kit, I'm not into girls.'

'Then why do you spoil things for Ti?' Kit returned quietly. 'I've seen you, Stu. Any man's interested in her and you're there, putting the boot in.'

'Really?' Stu arched a brow. 'I wonder if Ti feels I'm inhibiting her sex life. Shall we ask her?...Ti?'

'Stop this, Stu.' Ti knew he had her against the ropes.

'Then tell him,' Stu countered, 'or I will.'

'Tell me what?' Kit's eyes moved between their tense, angry faces.

'Leave it, Stu!' Tiree hated him at that moment.

'Why should I?' Stu threw back. 'I'm not the villain of the piece. You're the one playing with the stupid bastard's affections.'

'Ti?' Kit looked across the table at her, waiting for her to deny it.

Tiree would have if she could, but Stu was bound to contradict her, and perhaps she *had* been playing with Kit, allowing him to believe he stood a chance with her.

'Face it, bro,' Stu ran on, 'I'd sleep with you before Ti would. Pity you're not gay, isn't it?' he added with a slightly suggestive lift.

It wasn't the first time he'd ragged Kit in this manner, just the first time Kit had exploded.

'I am not gay!' he flung at Stu, and, jumping out of his chair, looked ready for a fight.

Stu barely turned a hair, enjoying the confusion he'd caused and, by remaining seated, made it almost impossible for Kit to hit him.

'That's what I said, wasn't it?' he appealed to Ti.

But Ti was more concerned about Kit, his face a mask of frustrated anger as he clenched and unclenched his fists before he finally decided to walk away.

She threw Stu an accusing glare, then followed Kit out into the hall where he was already shrugging into his bike leathers.

'Where are you going?' she asked in alarm.

'Nowhere,' he replied, even as he continued to zip up his jacket.

'You mustn't let Stu wind you up,' she ran on. 'It's just his way. You know that. He does it to everybody.'

'Yeah, well, I'm not gay,' Kit repeated as if it was the one fact that was really important to him.

Stu had definitely hit a nerve. It made Tiree wonder.

But she said, 'I know you're not,' because that's what he wanted to hear.

'I *would* have done something,' he insisted, 'if you'd been willing… He's right about that, though. You're not interested in me, are you? That was all in my head.'

'I do like you,' Tiree stressed, touching his arm. 'Please stay, Kit.'

'And if I do?' He waited for her to offer him something to stay for.

But Tiree couldn't. She didn't love him.

He took his answer in her silence and, grabbing his helmet, walked out into the night.

Stu appeared in the doorway to drawl, 'He's forgotten his mobile,' picking up the phone from where Kit had left it on the hall stand.

'Go after him, Stu,' she appealed. 'Stop him from doing anything stupid.'

Stu's mouth quirked. 'And why would I want to do that?'

It made Ti finally lose her temper. If he wanted reasons, she'd given them to him all right.

'Because you damn well caused this to happen,' she accused, 'and because you like Kit, I know you do. And because you're actually a good person when you're not being a total pig. And because I'm telling you to… Any of the above reasons will do.'

'The Mouse that roared,' Stu said as he had all those years ago, but he was already at the door, leaving her to follow.

Unfortunately they were seconds too late, as Kit roared out of the gate on his superbike. Stu hurried to unlock his car and slip behind the wheel.

'I'll come with you.' Ti went to climb in beside him.

'No, stay. I'll catch up with him, no problem,' Stu grinned, already revving his car up.

'Be careful, then.'

'For myself or him?'

'Him,' Ti replied shortly, then, for some reason, relented. 'Okay, you, too.'

'I know you love me really.' Those were the last words Stu ever said to her.

As hers were, 'I know you love me, too,' before he roared away into the night.

Ti didn't tell Sinclair the last part. She didn't expect him to understand her love for Stu. It was enough that he knew the rest.

'So you see,' she concluded at his lengthening silence, 'you were right, after all. It was my fault Kit died.'

Sinclair began to shake his head but she was looking down at the table and didn't see the gesture. 'How is it your fault, Ti? You weren't on that road.'

'I put them there.' She'd been living with the guilt ever since. 'Kit wouldn't have left if I'd tried harder to persuade him to stay.'

'You weren't responsible, Ti.' Sinclair rose to come round to her side and, lifting her from the chair, put his arms round her. 'You helped Kit kick his drug habit which is more than I did, and you were kind to him, that's all. If he made more of it than there was, that's to do with Kit, not you, and it's probably down to me and his mother and all the other adults who made a mess of his life.'

Ti was the one to shake her head now, refusing to let him take the blame. 'It was me. I should have made Stu stay away. I knew what he'd be like.'

'Do you think he forced Kit off the road?' Sinclair wondered if that was another thing on her conscience.

'I don't know,' Ti answered honestly. 'I hope not.'

'You loved him?' he asked as he had once before.

She nodded. 'No one else did. He wouldn't let them.'

'Then we both lost someone that was important to us,' Sinclair added. 'Just please, Ti, don't allow it to keep us apart.'

'You still want to marry me?' Tiree had thought her story would ruin any chance of a happy ever after.

'What do you think?' His smile was wry, but his eyes were serious, and in their steady blue gaze, Tiree saw her love reflected back at her so completely, she felt foolish for ever doubting it.

He knew the worst, and still he wanted her. He saw the best, and didn't try to change her. He accepted her for who she was and made her feel truly loved for the first time in her life.

Sinclair had done this before. He knew the routine. Rhys was by his side, patting his pocket, wearing a grin. Same as last time.

His collar chafed against his neck. No change there.

He still felt faintly ridiculous in tops and tails.

Then the music started up and his head turned and she blew all the cynicism away. Left was the wonder of how beautiful his bride was, in white lace and pearls, and how happy she'd made him and his daughter, smiling widely as she followed closely behind.

The vows he spoke were a solemn promise, this time in the certainty that he would keep them, and love and honour this girl until death did them part.

And Tiree echoed him word for word while her heart took flight.

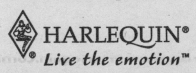

If you enjoyed what you just read,
then we've got an offer you can't resist!

Take 2 bestselling love stories FREE!

Plus get a FREE surprise gift!

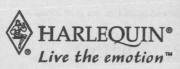

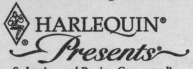

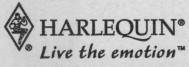